He wanted her. She knew, because the hunger in his gaze matched her own.

"I don't do this." The deep rumble of his voice sent a cascade of tiny earthquakes through her.

"Do what?" she asked.

"Kiss women I'm not in a relationship with."

"Are you kissing someone?"

"Only if she says I can. May I?"

She answered by leaning into his space on the bench and pressing her lips against his.

This was unwise. They both still wore their masks. She didn't know his name. She didn't know anything about him, except that he was a guest at the gala. He could be—

But then his strong hands reached out and pulled her to him and that tiny part of her shut up.

Dear Reader,

San Francisco is one of my favorite cities, and the Ferry Building is one of my favorite places to visit. On a recent visit, I noticed the staircase that leads up from the street to the upper level and thought it would be the perfect setting for Cinderella to lose a slipper...

Nelle Lassen doesn't lose her shoe, nor does she flee down a staircase, but the Ferry Building and the loss of an accessory (not to mention her heart) feature in this Cinderella-inspired story. Nelle is doing her best to reinvent herself after an emotionally devastating setback. The last thing she needs is to run into Grayson Monk—a member of a prominent Californian political dynasty running for Congress and, closer to home, the son of the man who ruined her father.

Grayson has his own problems, not the least of which is his half sister Finley, who believes Grayson needs a girlfriend—if only temporarily.

Then Nelle and Grayson are both invited to a masquerade ball...

I have a very soft spot for Nelle, who finds herself examining family lore she's always taken as fact, and I thoroughly enjoyed writing the sibling connection between Grayson and Finley. Families can be complicated and what we take as truths can be tangled, but love, as always, wins out.

I had a lot of fun writing *Cinderella Unmasked* and I hope you will have fun with Nelle and Grayson's story, too.

Happy reading!

Susannah

SUSANNAH ERWIN

CINDERELLA UNMASKED

HARLEQUIN®
DESIRE™

Recycling programs
for this product may
not exist in your area.

ISBN-13: 978-1-335-20930-6

Cinderella Unmasked

Copyright © 2020 by Susannah Erwin

This edition published by arrangement with Harlequin Books S.A.

For questions and comments about the quality of this book, please contact us at CustomerService@Harlequin.com.

Harlequin Enterprises ULC
22 Adelaide St. West, 40th Floor
Toronto, Ontario M5H 4E3, Canada
www.Harlequin.com

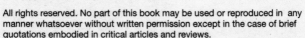

A lover of storytelling in all forms, **Susannah Erwin** worked for major film studios before writing her first novel, which won RWA's Golden Heart® Award. She lives in Northern California with her husband and a very spoiled but utterly delightful cat.

Books by Susannah Erwin

Harlequin Desire

Wanted: Billionaire's Wife
Cinderella Unmasked

Visit her Author Profile page at Harlequin.com, or susannaherwin.com, for more titles.

You can also find Susannah Erwin on Facebook, along with other Harlequin Desire authors, at Facebook.com/harlequindesireauthors!

For Barbara Ankrum, the best teacher and mentor a romance novelist could ever have.

One

Nelle Lassen gripped the full skirt of her silver-and-turquoise ball gown as one strappy, high-heeled sandal landed on the first step of the stone staircase outside San Francisco's historic Ferry Building. Then she pulled her foot back.

If she turned around now, she could go home. Take off the borrowed finery and slip into her comfy leggings and favorite hoodie. Curl up on the sofa with her laptop open to her social media accounts and her TV streaming the latest British costume drama. It was just the way she liked to spend her free evenings.

Or at least the way she used to like spending them, before her life was turned upside down and then shot out of a cannon to splat against a brick wall. Her reputation had been blackened, her career wiped from existence, her self-confidence eroded like a sandcastle during high tide. It had taken her a few months to devise a way forward and she still had far to go, but thanks to her best friend and roommate, Yoselin Solero, she'd checked off two major hurdles: new job, new city. And to go with them, a new name: Nelle, short for her given name, Janelle.

A chime came from a hidden pocket underneath the layers of tulle and lace, and she dug out her phone. "I'm at the gala," she answered.

"Inside?" Yoselin asked.

Nelle put both feet on the step. "I'm on the property."

"Get up those stairs," Yoselin commanded.

Nelle laughed. "Are you spying on me?"

Two flights above her, the silhouette of a figure wearing a pirate hat and a billowy blouse over knee breeches appeared. "Yes," Yoselin said into the phone, then lifted her hand and waved. "Hurry up! It's cold outside. I'll wait for you inside the door."

As if in response to Yoselin's words, a breeze blew across Nelle's cheeks. She shivered. The calendar said late June, but winds off the bay meant San Francisco could be wintry even in high summer. She took a deep breath, bracing salt air filling her lungs. The first real test of Project New Nelle would come at the top of the stairs.

She squared her shoulders. One small step to take, but it would be a giant leap forward into her new life. Not even Yoselin knew what a big jump it would be. It had taken all the strength Nelle had to smile and say yes to attending when she learned tonight's gala would be honoring Grayson Monk, venture capitalist, philanthropist, and the subject of several breathless media profiles that started off praising his business acumen but ended up extolling his athletic physique, blond-surfer good looks and piercing dark eyes.

Grayson Monk, the son of the man who'd nearly destroyed her father.

Her phone rang again, and she laughed. "Almost there," she said and clicked Disconnect. She was being ridiculous. She was in San Francisco, not New York City. She now worked in fundraising for a children's charity, not personal financial planning for a boutique firm like she had back East. She was an invited guest, not the disgraced target of a jealous coworker who was also her ex. There was no need to fear anyone at the ball. Grayson Monk included.

No matter what their family history was.

She started up the stairs, her heels clicking with purpose. As she neared the top, she caught a glimpse of the decorated venue and a gasp of amazement escaped her. "I'm not in Kansas anymore," she whispered under her breath. "This would be amazing even for Oz."

The Ferry Building was a historic Beaux Arts structure, one of the few survivors of the 1906 earthquake and fire that had destroyed most of San Francisco. Its grand hall was a wide, rectangular concourse interrupted in the center by an atrium that allowed guests to look down on the market stalls below. The ceiling soared high above her head, the barrel-shaped steel supports dotted with bright, globe-shaped lights. There were also enormous half-moon windows covered by latticework that resembled rows of stars. The mosaic tile floor was dotted with cocktail tables draped in festive colors, matching the bright costumes of the mingling guests exchanging conversation and laughter. A stage set with a podium and various musical instruments occupied one end of the hall, with a space in front of it left clear for dancing. The theme of the masquerade was "Venice by the Bay," and flowers, twinkling fairy lights and shimmering cloth drapes completed the transformation from staid city landmark into a festive, carnival-inspired dreamscape.

Yoselin waved her over to the check-in table, her dark eyes sparkling behind a black half mask decorated with white skulls and crossbones. She looked like Captain Jack Sparrow, if Jack had been a woman with golden brown skin and tousled mahogany curls. "Finally. I was beginning to wonder if your shoes were glued to the stairs. The speeches are about to start, and I'll point out who is who."

The woman seated behind the table smiled at them, a pen poised above her clipboard. "Welcome to the Peninsula Society's Carnival by the Bay! May I have your names?"

"We're guests of Octavia Allen," Yoselin responded. Octavia was on the board of directors of Create4All, where both Yoselin and Nelle worked. It had been her brainstorm for the two to attend the gala in the hopes of garnering more money for the children's nonprofit. As the executive director, Yoselin had been invited to help Mrs. Allen charm their current donors into increasing their pledges while Nelle, as the new development director, was tasked with bringing in sizable donations from people who had previously resisted Mrs. Allen's arm-twisting.

The woman's smile deepened as she made a check mark. "Mrs. Allen is already here. You'll be seated at her table. Number seventeen, the first row in front of the stage to the right." She looked up at Nelle and her gaze sharpened. "Did you bring your mask?"

Nelle held it up. The children who took art classes at Create4All had decorated every last millimeter of the plain half-mask bought at a party store. Silver sequins, opalescent crystals and seed pearls created an ocean-inspired fantasy that made up in exuberance what it lacked in sophistication.

"How…original," the woman said. "Don't forget, guests are asked to maintain the masquerade until the party ends at midnight."

"And then we turn back into our everyday pumpkin selves," Nelle said to Yoselin.

Yoselin laughed. "Let's find Octavia and the open bar. Not necessarily in that order." She strode into the party, her sword swinging in its scabbard at her side.

Nelle put on her mask, took a deep breath and followed in her friend's wake.

Grayson Monk waited in the wings of the make-shift stage and listened to the crowd noises coming from the other side of the heavy velvet curtains. The gala seemed to be going well. The food was top-notch, provided by world-renowned chefs. The wine and champagne as excellent as one would expect from Napa's and Sonoma's best vineyards. The crowd was glittering, the conversation scintillating, and smiles were plentiful. In short, it was what he'd come to expect from a Peninsula Society event. The usual.

But something was different. Off. What was it?

It took him a minute to realize the difference was him.

Previously he viewed his attendance at the annual gala as part of the cost of doing business in Silicon Valley. Anyone who was somebody—and those who wanted to be somebodies—made it a point to show their faces at the party. And not to be egotistical, but he knew they were there in part because they wanted his attention. Hungry entrepreneurs, hungry investors: they all hoped to dine off the high returns of Monk Partners, the private equity firm he'd founded right after graduating from Stanford.

Tonight, however, would change all that.

"Ladies and gentlemen, our philanthropist of the year, Grayson Monk!" Applause sounded, and a young man wearing a headset motioned for Grayson to make his entrance.

He strode onto the stage and shook hands with the Peninsula Society's president and gala chairperson. Then he faced the crowd, and after thanking the society and complimenting them on a successful evening, took a deep breath and went directly to the reason why he'd agreed to accept the award.

The speech.

"As some of you know, I've managed Monk Partners for the last fifteen years. We're proud of our record of helping the audacious and the intrepid build industry-leading companies. Some of today's biggest names in technology received the capital they required to become the successes they are from us. Like our most recent unicorn, Medevco, which under Luke Dallas and Evan Fletcher's leadership has changed the medical technology industry as we know it. And we're more than honored to give back to the community we're privileged to call home."

He swallowed. So far, so boilerplate. These were words he'd said a hundred times over, at various events and conferences. The next part of his speech, however...

"But all good things must come to an end at some point. So, with the permission of the Peninsula Society to take advantage of my brief moment in the spotlight, I'm announcing I'm stepping down from Monk Partners."

Audible gasps echoed in the cavernous space. Grayson held up his hands and smiled. "Hey, don't worry, Monk Partners is still in the same smart, savvy hands as before. Philip Adebayo will be taking over for me, with the rest of the team remaining in place. They're as committed as ever to the firm, our portfolio companies and our limited partners." He paused. "They might change the name, however."

That got him some laughs. Not many, but a few. He relaxed. The worst was over. It was like pulling a plastic bandage off—it stung for a second, but the anticipation of the announcement had been worse than the reality.

Of course, now he had to deal with the fallout. "I know you all want to get back to the party, so I'm going to leave it there. If you have questions, my office is more than prepared to take them in the morning—"

"What are you going to do next?" The shouted question came from the back of the room. Grayson held his right hand to his forehead to shield his eyes from the lights as he tried to focus on the crowd. But even if he could see the questioner, the masks made it difficult to tell who was who.

"I see someone can't wait until morning." He smiled. "I believe most people know my father recently had a serious health scare. I know it's a cliché, but I'm going to focus on family for the near future."

He paused, expecting to receive muted murmurs of understanding. After all, spending time with family was often used by CEOs and others as an excuse when their professional lives took unforeseen swerves. But the crowd's reaction was subdued, the chatter so light he could make out individual words. Including a snippet of conversation coming from a table near the stage.

"—eah, right, focus on family. Focus on taking over the family seat in Congress is more like it. But El Santo doesn't need another Monk in Congress. The people deserve better than—"

Then the crowd noise surged, and the rest of the words were lost.

He blinked. The voice was feminine. Young-sounding. And…hostile. Very hostile.

That was not the reaction he expected.

"So, um." Damn it. He never fumbled for words. He cleared his throat to cover his confusion. "I'll miss every single one of you—well, maybe not you, Vikram and Helen." He pointed at where he knew his fiercest competitors were standing, and the crowd laughed. He relaxed. He was back on track. "Although I will miss how you both kept me on my toes. But as everyone in this room knows, start-ups are pretty common. Fathers are one of a kind. Thank you for the award, but most of all, thank you for your friendship and support."

Applause, accompanied by chatter, bounced off the stone floor and high ceilings, filling the room. Grayson gave a short wave and returned to the backstage area, glad to see who else was there. There was a reason he'd mentioned Medevco in his speech. Not only was it his most profitable investment, but the two men running the company had become his closest friends in the year since he suggested they work together. He was even happier to see that one of them, Luke Dallas, had a highball glass containing two fingers of whisky waiting for him.

"Congratulations," Luke said, handing him the drink.

Grayson downed the dark amber spirits, his adrenaline ebbing as the alcohol sent warmth flowing through his veins. "On the award? It half belongs to your wife. She was the one who bargained a half hour of your time if I matched her donation to the society at last year's gala."

"I'm happy to let you have the award." Luke's wife, Danica, appeared at her husband's side. "After all, I have Luke." The two smiled at each other, oblivious to everyone else in their vicinity.

Even though Luke and Danica had been married for over a year, it still stunned Grayson a little to see the taciturn Luke be so open with his emotions. True, Danica was a great partner for him. Smart, highly capable and attractive, she and Luke just…clicked. Like LEGO pieces you might not think go together at first, but join to create a solid structure.

Luke was lucky he'd found his complement in Danica. Grayson wasn't sure he would ever find his. And he wouldn't settle for anything less than permanent. Casual dating didn't work for him.

Not that he was looking. Especially not now.

"Luke meant congratulations on being the sole topic of conversation for the evening. You're all anyone wants to talk about." Evan Fletcher, Luke's partner in Medevco, joined the small group. He handed a glass of water to Danica, keeping a very full stem of red wine for himself. "I could barely make it backstage, so many people wanted to stop and talk about you and your announcement. As soon as you step outside these curtains, prepare to be pounced upon."

Grayson stared at the bottom of his glass. Why hadn't someone invented a perpetually refilling whisky tumbler? He would invest in it. "And so it begins," he said into the glass.

Evan took a sip of wine and made a face. "What begins? Your retirement at age thirty-five? Living the dream, my friend. Please tell me you're buying an island with room for a guest. Who would happen to be me."

Grayson shook his head. "I'm not retiring. Not the way you think."

"Then why the whole…" Evan waved the hand holding the wine, causing it to come dangerously close to the rim. A few drops splashed over and landed on the floor.

Grayson eyed him. "Are you going to drink that, or just use it as a threat?"

"What do you mean—oh." Evan looked at his glass, and then glanced around for a place to put it down. He settled on the low table next to the sofa. "Next year, I want to be on the gala committee so I can choose the vintage."

"I want Grayson to answer Evan's question. If you're not retiring, then why the announcement?" Luke frowned in Grayson's direction. "Retirement is the logical explanation why you would walk away at the top of your game."

He might as well tell them. It wasn't as if this would be a secret for much longer. "This isn't for public consumption. Not yet, anyway. But my father is about to announce his resignation from Congress. And when he does, it will trigger a special election to fill the seat for the rest of his term. There's over a year left in it." He inhaled, the burn of the whiskey nothing but a fond memory. "And I'll be running."

Danica gasped, while Luke grinned and shook Grayson's hand. "Congrats. You have our support, of course. Although you could have let us know."

"To be honest, I'm surprised you're surprised." Whoever he'd overheard in the audience certainly wouldn't be. "It's always been my intention to follow my father into politics."

"Hello, hello!" The cheery greeting came from behind them. Grayson turned to see Bitsy Christensen, the gala chairwoman, bustling into the backstage area with her ever-present phone in her hand. Behind her followed several people carrying musical instruments.

"I thought for sure you'd all be sampling the food stations by now." Bitsy indicated the musicians. "The band needs to set up, so I'm afraid we have to take over this space."

"Of course." Grayson motioned for Luke and Danica to go ahead of him, and then turned to usher Evan out. Evan bent to pick up his glass of wine. Bitsy looked down to scroll through her phone.

The next few seconds played out in slow motion.

Evan moved toward the exit, frowning into his wine glass. Bitsy walked farther into the backstage area, fully engrossed in her screen. Neither of them looked up to see where they were going. Until they collided. Right in front of Grayson.

The phone sailed into the air. So did the glass of wine.

Grayson dove and caught the phone before it could hit the stone floor. Unfortunately, the wine hit him.

His white tuxedo shirt became splotchy pink. His black jacket and tie showed no damage, but he smelled as if he had bathed in a barrel of Napa's finest.

There was no way he could go out and face a room full of the Bay Area's brightest and smartest—all curious about the bombshell he'd dropped—appearing as if he'd just gone on the bender of all time backstage. He tried to blot the stains on his shirt with a paper cocktail napkin, but it was useless. The wine had soaked through the fabric to his skin.

"Oh, dear!" Bitsy appeared glued to the floor. "Oh, dear," she continued to repeat, as if on a loop.

"I'll ask the catering staff if they have dish towels," Evan volunteered. He disappeared behind the curtains.

Bitsy shook herself out of her shock. She took the phone Grayson held out to her and began to scroll through the screen. "We have extra costumes," she said. "In case someone forgot this was a masquerade. Always be prepared, right?" She fixed Grayson with an assessing stare, then fired off a text. "My assistant will be right here. I told her the Pierrot ensemble would be best, as it will hopefully accommodate your frame."

Pierrot? Great. Just how he wanted to appear to people he would soon be hitting up for campaign donations. A clown in baggy white pajamas.

He found a corner out of the way of the musicians and waited for the costume to arrive, his mind going over his goals for the rest of the night: talk to potential campaign donors, reassure nervous investors about his departure and—

"The people of El Santo deserve better."

The overheard words looped in his head, like the hook of a pop song turned earworm, despite his best efforts to concentrate on other thoughts.

Sure, there were people out there who were less than pleased with him. The entrepreneurs whose pitches he'd declined. The CEOs whose companies weren't right for an acquisition offer. His last girlfriend, who didn't appreciate having their week in Bali cut short by five days because he had to fly home to save a deal.

But in general, Grayson enjoyed a good working relationship with people. He'd been a leader since childhood, when he anchored his ten-and-under swimming relay team to a state championship. He'd started his own small venture capital fund in high school as a way to fund his swim meets, and when he decided to give up the pool, his skill at persuading entrepreneurs to work with him had led to the formation of Monk Partners. Now it had one of the best track records in Silicon Valley of picking winning investments.

But he'd always known he would follow his father into public service. It was the family tradition, after all. His great-grandfather had been Governor of California. His grandfather sat on the state supreme court. Taking over his father's seat in the House of Representatives would be the culmination of everything he had been raised to be.

The costume arrived neatly packaged in a clear plastic bag, breaking his reverie. Grayson took out a billowing white tunic, loose drawstring trousers and a tall cone hat. The outfit was even more ridiculous than he imagined. He was halfway to shoving the articles back into the bag, a wine-soaked shirt preferable to looking like a literal clown, when his hands stilled.

This was a rare opportunity. The next months were going to be a whirlwind of meetings and paperwork, shaking hands and kissing babies. His social life, which he already kept on the light and noncommittal side due to his long work hours, would become nonexistent. And if he won…well, he would have to say goodbye to the concept of taking time for himself.

A head-to-toe costume was the last thing anyone would expect to him to wear. It would allow him relative anonymity to spend time with his friends and enjoy a night out without worrying about, as Evan put it, being pounced on. There would be plenty of time to answer people's questions about the transition at Monk Partners next week.

Tonight was his for the taking. One last evening of freedom.

And maybe he could discover why someone had publicly voiced the concern he carried deep inside.

The guests seated with Nelle and Yoselin at Mrs. Allen's table burst into animated chatter as soon as Grayson Monk left the stage. Only Nelle stayed quiet, sipping her cranberry juice and vodka, hoping the ice in her drink would cool the heat still present in her cheeks.

She'd seen recent photos of Grayson, of course. Even caught a few of his television appearances. Who hadn't? He'd been a darling of the media since he made his first billion eight years ago at the tender age of twenty-five. But he was taller and broader in real life than any two-dimensional image could convey. Nor could the cameras capture the intensity in his gaze, the charm in his smile.

A deep flush filled every pore of her skin when he'd turned that smile in her direction. She knew he only looked her way because the man who had shouted out the question sat several tables behind her. But his sheer charisma had hit her like a tsunami, much to her chagrin. She held on to the knowledge that no matter how likable and charming he may seem when giving a speech, she knew the truth. It was a front so he could get what he wanted when he wanted, no matter the collateral damage.

Like father, like son.

And anyway, not that she would ever be this close to him again. She could start to relax and enjoy the evening. Now that she knew he was wearing a tuxedo, his dark blond hair uncovered by a mask or hat, it would be easy to spot him—and avoid his general vicinity.

Yoselin ended her conversation with the man on her left and turned to Nelle. "Is he really going to run?"

"Who?" Nelle widened her eyes, crossing her fingers Yoselin was talking about anyone else but the subject of Nelle's thoughts.

Yoselin indicated the stage, where musicians were now setting up additional instruments. "Grayson Monk. For Congress."

At the rate her drink was disappearing, Nelle was going to need a refill soon. Maybe two. "I guess? I wouldn't know."

"But you grew up in El Santo, right? I forgot until you mentioned he's from there, too," Yoselin persisted.

Nelle shook her head, aware her cheeks probably still matched the color of her drink. "I did, but he's several years older. Besides, we ran in different social circles. And speaking of running, did I tell you I want to run a marathon this year—"

Mrs. Allen leaned over the table. "Did you say you grew up with Grayson Monk?"

Nelle choked on a piece of ice. After coughing, she met Mrs. Allen's curious gaze. "We're from the same town. But—"

"Excellent!" Mrs. Allen clapped her hands together, her rings catching the glow of the stage lights and throwing small prisms of color onto the table. "I've been trying to secure Grayson as a key sponsor for eons. With his support, we are sure to receive the financing necessary for the East Bay facility." She nodded at Nelle. "I knew there had to be a reason why Yoselin demanded we hire you."

Nelle bit her lip and looked down at the table. What Mrs. Allen said was true: Yoselin had had to fight hard to hire her. Mrs. Allen in particular wanted another candidate, one with deep connections to the Bay Area's elite.

"There are many reasons why Nelle is perfect for the job." Yoselin held out her left hand and started to tick them off on her fingers. "One, she—" Her words trailed off as she spotted a tall black man wearing a judge's robe with a white collar and sporting a plain half mask making his way toward their table. "Jason!"

Jason grinned, and Yoselin got up out of her chair so she could kiss her boyfriend. "What are you doing here? I thought you couldn't be my date because you had study group after torts class," she said, somewhat out of breath.

"I can take one night off studying." He smiled and intertwined his hands with hers. "I borrowed an old robe from Judge Durham, and Mrs. Allen left me a ticket so I could surprise you."

Yoselin smiled at Mrs. Allen. "Thank you."

Mrs. Allen waved her hands in dismissal. "You've been working so hard it's the least I could do." She smiled at Nelle. "And now that I know that Nelle has a connection to Grayson Monk, I'm even happier. You two have fun. Nelle and I will take care of business."

The musicians took their spots and started to warm up. The room dimmed as streamers of purple, green and blue light shot outward from the proscenium outlining the stage. Jason held out his hand to Yoselin. "Shall we?"

Yoselin turned to Nelle. "You'll be okay if I leave you here?"

"Of course she will," Mrs. Allen stated. "She's with me."

"Farmer's market this Sunday, right, Nelle?" Jason asked. "Can't go to brunch afterward without you."

"It's on my calendar." Nelle smiled as she watched the couple walk toward the dance floor. Yoselin and Jason looked so…complete. A unit. And she appreciated the invitation. But while they never made her feel like the third wheel, she was well aware she was the odd woman out in their world built for two.

It might be nice to have someone of her own to put his arms around her, to sway with on the dance floor and laugh at a shared joke as Yoselin and Jason were doing right that minute.

It *might be.*

But first, she needed to make Project New Nelle a success. Put solid ground under her feet. Rebuild her reputation, career, confidence. Once she had her life back in order, maybe she could think about finding a partner to share it.

She caught Mrs. Allen's gaze and put on her best professional smile. "I'm here for work, so feel free to point me in the right direction."

Mrs. Allen glanced around the room, and then her face lit up. "Ah! There's Bitsy, by the other side of the stage. But I should speak to her alone. Why don't you mingle? We'll meet back here shortly." She rose from her seat and slipped on her phoenix mask, complete with towering red and gold feathers that shot toward the vaulted ceiling.

The other guests at the table also started to leave,

some heading for the dance floor, others for the buffet tables and open bars dotting the perimeter of the hall. Nelle weighed her options and decided people were more likely to chat with a stranger if they had drinks in their hands instead of food on their forks. She fought her way through the crowd already forming at the nearest bar.

"Cranberry and soda, please," she said to the bartender, once she managed to get his attention. The vodka from her last drink was still making her head swim. Then she turned back to scan the concourse, hoping to keep an eye on Mrs. Allen so she could time her arrival back at the table to coincide with hers. But she didn't see her hostess in the sea of black tuxedos, brilliantly bright gowns and multihued costumes.

"Here you go," the bartender announced. Nelle turned around to reach for her drink. A sharp elbow landed in her side, causing her to stumble against the bar. Her fingers slid against the glass, sending it spinning down the polished, slick surface. It was headed toward a guest with his back to her. He was wearing a blinding white costume and was oblivious to the disaster heading his way. She opened her mouth to warn him—

—when he turned, assessed the situation with one split-second glance, and caught the glass. Not a drop spilled.

He glanced to his left and his right. When he saw Nelle staring at him, her mouth still open in shock, he smiled. "Yours?" he asked, indicating the glass.

He was tall, well over six feet. Although he was

dressed like a Venetian clown in a loose white top, his broad shoulders could not be hidden. Physically imposing men usually made Nelle wary, but there was something—perhaps the twinkle of humor in the dark eyes behind the mask, perhaps the way the one-sided smile gave him a slightly self-deprecating air—that allowed her to let down her guard. She smiled back. "Guilty," she responded. "That was some catch."

"One out of two isn't bad. I hope I don't have to go for three." He handed her the drink, careful not to let go until she had a firm grip on the glass. Their fingers brushed, just for a second, but long enough for a jolt of electricity to shock her into awareness. "This isn't the first drink thrown at me tonight."

Six months ago, she would have politely smiled and then walked away, secure in her staid but comfortable relationship. But Mrs. Allen had told her to mingle, didn't she? And while the old Janelle didn't flirt, she decided—spurred on by the lingering vodka mixed with his lingering touch—that Nelle did. She raised an eyebrow and leaned, ever so slightly, into his space. "Intriguing. Although in my case, it was an accident, I didn't throw it. What did you do to earn a drink thrown at you?"

"I tried to save a phone in distress."

"And the phone threw a drink at you in return? There really is an app for everything."

He laughed. It was a good laugh. A rumble of warm bass notes that resonated deep inside, the vibrations loosening the steel bands that kept her physical response to attractive men locked up tight. She couldn't help but grin in response, and his dark eyes took on a new light of appreciation as their gazes met and caught. He angled his body toward hers. "I was hoping for a bottomless whisky tumbler earlier tonight, but an app that throws drinks might be the idea the world is missing."

"Why stop at drinks? There are so many possibilities! Like, tomatoes."

"Tomatoes?"

"For, say, a bad movie. You could virtually throw a tomato at it."

"I think that app already exists. In a way. Rotten Tomatoes?"

She nodded. "Oh, right. So how about an app for... wedding cake?"

"Wedding cake?"

"You know, when the bride and groom cut the cake, and they feed it to each other but sometimes they purposefully miss and the cake is smeared all over? What if bridal couples could use an app instead? Think of the dry cleaning costs it would save."

His teeth flashed white in a very appealing smile. "You must go to very messy weddings. Did that happen at yours?"

She held up her bare left hand. "Not yet, and hopefully not ever. It's not my idea of fun. The cake thing, I mean, not the wedding. That is something I do hope... I mean..." Her cheeks grew hot. What made her talk about weddings with a man she'd just met? "Um, what else can be thrown...? I know. Milkshakes."

"Technically, milkshakes are a drink."

She tsked. "It's not just a drink. A good milkshake glides over your tongue, creamy and rich. It's so thick you can't suck it through a straw despite pulling as hard as you can. The spoon stands straight up—" She stopped, suddenly aware they were standing very, very close. So close, the sequins covering her bodice almost brushed the white canvas of his top.

"Go on," he said, his voice low and verging on rough. "Describe what you do to the straw again?"

"The straw." She swallowed, her attention caught by his chin and lips, the part of his face fully visible. His chin was square, firm, clean-shaven. His lips were neither full nor thin. If she were Goldilocks, she would pronounce them "just right." She wondered… "The straw is—"

"There you are. I've been waiting at our table for you."

Mrs. Allen's voice came from behind her. Startled, Nelle stumbled and almost fell against the man. He steadied her with a light grip on her bare upper arm. His touch delivered a quick lightning bolt of pure current. But she didn't have time to dwell on it as Mrs. Allen was joining her at the bar.

The older woman settled her cool gaze on Nelle, still leaning slightly against her conversational partner. "Shall we? If now is a good time for you, that is."

Nelle pulled herself upright, a tense knot forming between her shoulders. Her first work assignment and she was already failing. Her new life would fall apart before it began. "Yes. Of course. I'll follow you."

It wasn't until Mrs. Allen had led her to the other side of the venue that she realized she hadn't said goodbye to the man with the perfect lips, much less remembered to take her drink with her.

Two

Grayson stared after the woman in the mermaid mask as she wove her way through the people clustered around the bar, tracing her movements until she was swallowed up by the crowd. He was intrigued by what he'd seen of her face, partially hidden though it was by the elaborate mask. Bee-stung lips, determined chin, sparkling light blue eyes that refracted light. And when he looked into those eyes, he could have sworn she was intrigued as well.

He'd had more than his share of casual encounters, enough to be bored with them. He didn't need to pick up women at bars, even an open bar at a charity gala. But he also could tell the difference between an encounter that inspired lust and nothing more, and one that intrigued his brain and soul as well as lower, less cognitively enabled parts of him.

"Who was that?" Evan managed to squeeze next to him at the bar. "Let me guess—an ex who realized it was you under the mask."

"Funny. But no. I take it you didn't recognize her, either?"

Evan shrugged. "I have a hard enough time with faces when people aren't covering them up. Tonight? Not my optimum environment." He peered closer at Grayson. "You okay? I really am sorry."

Grayson held up his left hand, dismissing Evan's concern, as he searched the crowd in a vain attempt to trace the woman's steps. "Apology accepted an hour ago."

Where was she? How could she disappear so fast?

"Not about spilling the wine. I'm sorry an attractive woman noped out on you. Welcome to how the rest of us live."

Grayson focused on his friend. "How do you know she's pretty? You've seen her without her mask? When? Where?" A surge of electricity ran through him. If Evan was holding out on him…

Evan grinned and saluted Grayson with his newly acquired drink. "I've never seen her before. But you obviously find her attractive. I haven't seen you this interested in ages. Go after her."

Grayson shrugged Evan's hand off. "She's so interested she left without her drink."

"So take her drink to her. Look at this crowd. It's

like a zombie flick, only they want alcohol instead of brains. You'd be a hero."

Grayson shifted on his feet. He should stay and talk to his colleagues and industry peers. He'd detonated the equivalent of an incendiary device with his announcement, and it was his responsibility to clean up any resulting damage. On the other hand, phones and email would still work on Monday.

He glanced at the crush of people hoping to take advantage of the open bar. Evan was right. Taking her drink to her would be the gentlemanly thing to do. He said goodbye to his smirking friend, picked up the abandoned glass and waded into the throng of the Bay Area's finest.

He started with the dance floor, literally heaving with gyrating bodies. The beat was fast and loud and thumped against the walls of his chest. Next he toured the concourse, not receiving a second glance from people who would normally have called him over to say hello or pitch him a new business idea. The costume definitely hid his identity. It was an odd but not unwelcome sensation to be this anonymous.

After several circuits, the glass was cold and slippery in his hand, the ice nearly all melted. He glanced at his watch and noticed it was nearing eleven o'clock. Maybe the person she briefly spoke to at the bar was her significant other. Maybe she'd already left the party with her partner. The thoughts made the whiskey in his stomach burn, and not in a good way.

Maybe the jolt of mutual appreciation when their gazes met had been all in his head.

He returned to the dance floor, intending to reveal himself to a group of investors in town from New York City who might be useful to cultivate, when a flash of silver and aqua dazzled his gaze.

He'd caught his mermaid.

She stood on the other side of the dance floor, her profile turned to him. Through the wall of dancers, he caught glimpses of details he missed during their first encounter: an hourglass waist defined by swirls of beads and pearls, full curves spilling over the strapless bodice, loosely braided chestnut hair wound with aqua and silver ribbons. A diadem of seashells and pearls crowned her head.

She turned and looked up. Their gazes met, held. He kept his steady, not ashamed to be caught admiring her. The connection he'd felt at the bar came roaring back, pinpricks of awareness coming alive all over his skin. No, he had not been imagining it. And she felt it, too. He could tell in the way she stood still, her gaze focused on his, her right hand pressing against the creamy skin of her throat.

The dancers disappeared. The entire Ferry Building faded away. They were the only two people in the entirety of the universe.

He smiled. And held up her glass, shaking it slightly. An answering smile curved her full lips, but she shook her head. The statuesque woman standing next to her in a phoenix costume followed her gaze and smiled, then said a few words to his mermaid, making shooing motions with her hands.

And his mermaid started to walk in his direction.

Did the crowd part for her? That was how he saw it. Or maybe it only seemed that way, the dancers melting to the sidelines as she advanced onto the dance floor. He met her halfway, the sharp shards of purple and red light turning to beams of soft blue as the band shifted from a pounding rock rhythm into a jazzy standard. The glow caused the pearls sewn on her dress to shimmer and made her appear even more like a mythological creature from the ocean depths. A sea goddess.

He swallowed, hoping to work moisture into his mouth. "You forgot this." He held out her drink.

"Oh. Thank you." She took it but made no attempt to take a sip. Their gazes continued to hold as the singer crooned about flying to the moon and playing with stars. She finally broke the silence between them. "Are you, um, trying to go two for three after all?" She punctuated the sentence with a breathy laugh.

He shook his head, uncomprehending, still marveling he had found her. Still enjoying the frisson of energy that melded their gazes together.

"The drink? Two out of three? Throwing it at you? Not that I want to throw it at you," she said in a rush. "I mean, from before? You said at the bar that was the second time, so—" She stopped, looked down at the glass, and then her lips formed a perfect circle. "Wait. The ice is melted. Have you been carrying this around the whole time?"

He gave a nonchalant shrug. Or at least he tried for nonchalant. "Have you seen the line for the bar?"

"You know there's more than one, right?" She cocked her head, her chestnut braid falling over her left shoulder. A dangling silver ribbon came to nestle in her generous cleavage.

He had never been so jealous of a sliver of fabric before.

"Multiple bars? Really?" He looked around the room. He had been so focused on finding her he had ignored the various food and, yes, bars set up around the concourse. "Huh." He indicated the drink. "Well. That should save you from fighting through the crowd for a while, at least."

"Very thoughtful. Even though accepting a strange drink at a party is definitely on the list of things women should never do."

He hadn't thought about that. "Of course. You're right. I can have guests here vouch for me if you want."

She smiled, a dimple appearing in her left cheek. The room seemed to spin around them with her as its axis. "Maybe I shouldn't, but I trust you. Thank you again." She turned to go back to her friends.

"Dance with me." The request left his mouth before he had a chance to think it through.

She stopped at the edge of the floor. "With a drink in my hand? You do like living dangerously when it comes to beverages."

He stepped to her side, took the glass from her unresisting grip and handed it to a passing waiter. "Problem solved."

"Hey! You just gave that back to me." She folded

her arms, but a smile played at the edges of her mouth. "And there's still a problem. I didn't say yes."

He held out his right hand. "Please. Dance with me?"

She regarded him, white teeth making an appearance to bite her lower lip. "Won't your date mind?"

He smiled. "No date. No significant other, here or anywhere. And you? Is someone waiting for you to come back?" *Please say no*, his brain chanted.

A sharp light flared in her gaze, and then she shook her head. Then she placed her hand in his. It was warm and soft, and her fingers wove into his like they were custom-made to fit.

The band's tempo decreased, the music changing from upbeat Sinatra to a lush ballad. She floated in his arms, her hands resting lightly on his shoulders, their movements in perfect sync. He held her waist, careful not to crush the beads and sequins, reveling in how her curves filled his palms. Their gazes met, and his stomach literally flipped. He didn't think such a thing physically possible.

He was not a romantic. Love at first sight was a creaky fairy tale no one over the age of twelve should believe. But when the song stopped, he didn't want his time with her to stop with it.

"Thank you. That was…thank you." Her hands dropped to her sides, but she didn't step out of the circle of his arms.

"You're welcome." He was vaguely aware they were the focus of curious stares. They stood still as the music segued into country-western pop and the other guests assembled for line dancing. They needed to either join them or leave the floor. "Are you—" he swallowed, his mouth as dry as the Mojave Desert "—are you hungry?"

Her gaze fell to his mouth, a split-second flash, before meeting his again. "Depends on what you mean," she said, her voice husky with amusement.

"Would you like to have dinner?" he clarified.

She glanced around. The buffet tables that had earlier overflowed with delicacies from around the Bay Area looked decidedly barren. "I would, but it's slim pickings."

He smiled. "I think I know just the thing. Any objections to pork, garlic or rice?"

Her stomach growled in response. The sound was unmistakable over the rhythmic stomping of the guests and the twanging guitar music. Her eyes widened in horror before they both broke into laughter. He held out his left arm to her. "Let's see if we can do something about that."

Nelle allowed him to guide her out of the building, not sure what had come over her. The vodka should have worn off long ago. And while there were plenty of guests dressed as mages and witches, she doubted she was under a spell. Unless the Ferry Building itself had ensorcelled her, the majesty of the old building, the brilliant costumes, and the artful decorations and lighting combining to sweep her into a waking dream. Even Mrs. Allen had conspired to make the evening magical, telling Nelle to go have an unforgettable night when she saw someone was waiting for her on the dance floor.

And the reason why she hoped the dream would continue: her companion. Was it bizarre, perhaps even perilous, to let a man whose name she still didn't know guide her out of the party without letting Yoselin or Mrs. Allen know she was leaving? Normally, she would be the first to say yes. He was still wearing his mask, even. They both were. Spending time with an unknown man in disguise hadn't worked out well for the heroine of *The Phantom of the Opera*.

The old her would have refused to go with him.

But Nelle had never been held on a dance floor like that before. As if she were something precious, something to be treasured and respected. The touch of his large hand curved around her waist was solid and reassuring. She didn't want to miss the chance to grip his impossibly broad shoulders again, or watch his bicep flex when he offered her his arm.

"Are we going far?" she asked. "Because I'll need to change shoes." She opened her handbag and pulled out her pair of emergency slippers, folded into a tight square.

He laughed, a warm reverberation that made her stomach flutter. "No. In fact—" he indicated an empty bench on the large plaza across the Embarcadero from the Ferry Building "—your dining venue awaits."

She raised her eyebrows, even though he wouldn't see her expression because of the mask. He held out his hand and she took it, proud that she kept the trembling to a minimum. He had barely settled her on the bench's cool wood slats before a young man ran up to them and handed him a large brown paper bag.

"That looked like a rather illicit transaction," she said.

He grinned and opened the bag, drawing out a large, heavy cylinder wrapped in shiny foil and handing it to her. "Tosilog burritos. They're only illegal if you're on a diet." He took a second foil-wrapped burrito out of the bag, followed by two bottles of sparkling mineral water. But when he went to take his mask off, she reached out to still his hand.

"I was told the rules of the ball were quite strict. No unmasking until the clock strikes midnight."

His beautifully shaped lips quirked upward and he let his hand fall. "So you're a rule follower."

"I—" She was about to say yes. But then she remembered it was Janelle who followed the rules. Janelle who thought if she did everything right and followed the straight and narrow path, the world would reward her for her faithfulness to its strictures. Janelle, who had been shockingly wrong. "So few things in life are truly mysterious," she ended up saying. "Why not enjoy this while it lasts? It's just for—" she glanced at the Ferry Building clock in its tower, high above them "—fifty more minutes."

"Fifty long minutes," he replied.

"Are you saying you can't last that long?" She traced the seam of her foil-wrapped burrito with her fingers, seeking the best place to unwrap it.

His gaze followed the path of her fingers, then it

rose and caught hers. "I'm coming to the conclusion delayed gratification might make the outcome even more satisfying."

She wet her lips, but whether in reaction to the heavenly smell of roasted pork and garlic or to his words, she wasn't sure. "Good things come to those who wait."

A dangerous, knowing smile curved his lips. "Good doesn't even begin to describe it."

She shivered, and it had nothing to do with the cool night air.

"You're cold." He started to look around as if to find a more sheltered spot.

"Maybe that's because I'm the only one sitting." She indicated the empty space on the bench next to her.

He smiled and sat down. Her full skirt threatened to spill over into his space and she gathered it up, noticing how the trousers of his costume drew tight over powerful, well-muscled thighs when he was seated. Was the rest of him as muscular—she quickly turned her head to take a bite of her burrito. And then another. The heavenly taste of marinated roasted pork and garlic rice took over her attention. But she remained aware of the solid heat of him pressed against her leg, the brush of his arm against her side.

They ate in companionable silence, breaking it occasionally to exchange observations about the people walking by. Their senses of humor meshed well, although his was much drier than hers, and laughter punctuated their sentences. Then soft chords of music began to fill the small pauses in their conversation. After a quick mental check to make sure she wasn't hallucinating a romantic soundtrack for the evening, she spotted the source. A piano on wheels sat in the middle of the plaza, played by a young man who had a hat out on the ground beside him to collect tips.

She started to laugh. It was perfect for this dreamy, incredible evening. Almost too perfect.

As if he had read her mind, her mysterious stranger said, "I was just thinking the only thing this moment lacked was a Chopin concerto."

"It is a bit too on the nose," she agreed, after swallowing the last bite of her burrito. "But appreciated. And speaking of appreciation, that was delicious. Excellent delivery service, too," she added, wiping her fingers on the napkin he provided.

"It's my favorite food in the city," he said. "I try other places, but I keep returning to this food truck. It's no milkshake, however." He looked at her, and his gaze sharpened. "You have something on your cheek. Here." He pointed to the spot on his own face.

She tried to remove the offending stain with her napkin. "Better?"

He shook his head. "No. May I?"

At her nod, he cupped her cheek to hold her head still. His fingers rested lightly on her skin, but they lit up her nervous system like a match to a trail of gasoline. Her hands began to tremble as he gently passed his napkin once, then twice, over the offending spot. The piano music soared into a crescendo, echoing her heartbeat.

"There," he said.

Her gaze caught his. The streetlight high above cast a halo around his peaked hat. His mask caused shadows to fall on his cheekbones, but she was close enough to see how the gold highlights in his whiskey-brown eyes shone.

For her.

He wanted her. She knew, because the hunger in his gaze matched her own. Simmering since their encounter at the bar, it now roared, demanding to be satiated.

"I don't do this." The deep rumble of his voice sent a cascade of tiny earthquakes through her.

"Do what?" she asked. It came out as a breathy croak.

"Kiss women I'm not in a relationship with."

"Are you kissing someone?"

"If she says I can. May I?"

She answered by leaning closer to him on the bench and pressing her lips against his.

This was unwise, the tiny part of her brain not occupied by kissing and being thoroughly kissed in return tried to warn her. They both still wore their masks. She didn't know his name. She didn't know anything about him, except that he was a guest at the gala. He could be married. He could be a serial killer. He could be—

But then his strong hands reached out and pulled her to him and that tiny warning voice shut up. She let the electricity that had been building around them all evening take over, opening her mouth to the sweep of his tongue, exploring his mouth in return. There was nothing sloppy or awkward about his kiss, nothing overly practiced, either. He knew exactly the best angle, the right amount of pressure. This was a master class in kissing and not a single cell of hers wanted to be left out of the lesson.

She wound her arms around his neck, holding him against her, not wanting to let him go when he pulled back, just enough to whisper against her lips, "I'm going to stand up."

But before she could make a sound of disapproval, he had stood up, tugged her up with him, then sat back down on the bench and pulled her down on top of his lap.

The layers of tulle she wore compressed to nothing, and the thin fabric trousers he wore were an equally inadequate barrier between them. His thighs were indeed as firm and muscled as they looked. And warm. So warm. She wanted to burrow in the heat they created together, the ravenous flames he coaxed into life with his lips and tongue consuming all rational thought.

She wound her arms around his neck, pressing her breasts against his hard-muscled chest. She had forgotten how delectable a kiss could be. Or maybe she never really knew before now.

The clock in the Ferry Building tower gave a deep, sonorous clang. Once, twice, ten more times. It was midnight.

She lifted her mouth from his, just an inch, the

effort taking enormous will. "The masquerade is officially over."

His gaze was dark and wild, but she could see it come into focus as he processed her words. "So it is."

"I guess that means…" She ran her fingers along the edge of his mask, across his cheekbones.

He drew in his breath, sharply. Then those firm, talented lips of his quirked upward. "I guess it does."

He untied the silver ribbons that held her handmade mask in place. She reached up and removed first his conical hat, already threatening to fall off, then slid the party store domino up and over his head.

Her gaze shifted to take in his entire face for the first time. And she froze.

She couldn't breathe. She couldn't move. She couldn't form thoughts, except for the one bouncing around her brain in a continuous loop.

She was kissing Grayson Monk.

Grayson's breath caught as he untied the mask, the silver ribbons slipping through his fingers as it fell to the ground.

She was beautiful.

But he already knew that, even before the mask came off. She was funny and charming, and time in her company sped by. The moments when conversation ceased and silence reigned weren't awkward, as they usually were when he just met someone, but comfortable, as if they'd known each other for a long time. Her beauty showed in her dry wit and breathy laughter, her sensuous lips that fit against his as if made for him and her mind-blowing kisses that made him forget his own name.

Now, without the mask, he could take in the rest of the perfection that was his sea goddess. Her aquiline nose, as regal as the rest of her. Her sharply angled eyebrows. Blue eyes the color of the Pacific immediately after the sunrise.

And she stared back at him in…horror. Shock. And loathing.

The antipathy in her gaze caused his arms to fall away from her soft curves. Without him supporting her, there was nothing keeping her anchored on his lap. She slid off in a cloud of tulle, nearly falling to the ground in her haste to put distance between them.

A chill cut through the passion keeping his brain pleasantly fogged. "Are you okay? Did I—if this was something you didn't want, I'm sorry—"

"You're Grayson Monk." Her voice was low, controlled, cool. Too cool, considering what they had been doing. She gathered her skirts in one hand and began to back away. "I… I have to go." Then she turned. Gathered her skirts. And started to run.

What the hell just happened? A few seconds ago, he was enjoying one of the most arousing moments of his life. Now this woman was literally running away, her face set in what could only be called horror.

He managed to catch the end of her stole, the flimsy fabric tangling in his fingers. It slipped from around her neck and she turned to grab at it. "Let go," she commanded.

"Don't leave like this. Talk to me." He handed the stole back to her.

She snatched it from him, balling it up in her hands. "There's nothing to say."

"I don't understand." She must have felt the same connection he did. Kisses like that were as rare as start-ups with ten-billion-dollar valuations. "Did I do something wrong? Tell me. I'll apologize. And it won't happen again."

She shook her head. Her gaze remained focused on the fabric tightly held in her grasp. "I made the mistake. But don't worry. This definitely won't happen again."

He opened his mouth. Closed it. Opened it again. "Do we know each other?"

She shook her head, even as he anticipated her answer. He knew they didn't. There was no way he would have forgotten her, for one. Then she glanced up at him. The streetlights above caught a wet shimmer in the corner of her eyes. "No."

Her gaze dropped. And before he could respond, she fled. There was no other word for it. She dashed across the plaza toward the front entrance of the Ferry Building, her diadem crooked and threatening to fall off. He started to follow her, but something white and sparkling near his shoe caught his attention.

Her mask. It must have slipped to the ground after he untied it. The pearls and crystals shimmered in the glow from the streetlight high above as he picked it up.

"Wait," he called after her. "You left this." This

close, he could see the crooked lines of glue and the exuberant use of glitter that made her mask one-of-a-kind. It deserved more than to be discarded on a San Francisco city sidewalk.

She didn't hear him—or didn't want to hear him. She continued to run, a flash of silver and aqua weaving around the people on the plaza. He started after her, but a streetcar pulled to a stop on the tracks running parallel to the Embarcadero and cut off his route. By the time he got around the obstacle, she had disappeared.

The only sign she had been there was her mask, still clutched tightly in his hands.

Three

Grayson pulled his Tesla Model S into the parking space in front of the low-slung wood-and-stucco building set back from the main road and hidden by pine trees and tall shrubs. Tourists taking a detour off the freeway on their way between San Jose and San Francisco might drive by and mistake the building for an insurance agency, or perhaps a dentist's office. Little would they know that money amounting to the GDP of several small nations flowed in and out of it on a daily basis.

His name was still on the small brass sign next to the front door. He smiled at it, then at the receptionist who waved a greeting as he passed through the security gate. His smile faltered when he saw who was waiting for him in the lobby.

Finley.

His older sister was on the phone, holding a softly murmured conversation while scrolling through social media accounts on a second phone. When she saw him, she ended her call and put both phones down. "We need to talk," she said.

"I thought we were going to talk next week." Grayson strode past her and down the hall. He unlocked the door at the end and ushered Finley, who had followed him, into the suite of rooms he used as his office. His assistant wasn't in yet, so he busied himself turning on lights and powering up his laptop.

Finley positioned herself on the sleek leather sofa that occupied one wall, stretching her arms along the back and crossing feet clad in Italian-made pumps at the ankle. As usual, not one dark hair was out of place on her head. Her elegant gray suit, no doubt hand-sewn in Hong Kong by her favorite tailor, was a stark contrast to Grayson's Silicon Valley uniform of dark blue jeans, crisp cotton button-down shirt and running shoes.

The product of a first, disastrous three-month marriage, Finley had been just shy of a year old when Barrett Monk married their mother. Grayson came along ten months later. The half siblings shared brown eyes and little else except for a devotion to the Monk name and legacy. In Grayson's case, it was his heritage and birthright. But he was glad Finley cared as deeply as she did, even though her last name remained Smythe. Barrett had never formally adopted Finley, though he remained her legal guardian after their mother died.

He blamed the demands of his political career for why the paperwork was never completed. Grayson didn't see that it mattered. She was his sister, nothing half about it.

Still, it didn't mean he was always happy to see her.

"I have a long day ahead of me," he told Finley. "We agreed I could take the necessary time to hand over Monk Partners to my team. What do you need?"

Finley brushed an imaginary piece of lint off her left trouser thigh. "I hear you had an interesting time at the Peninsula Society ball."

Grayson bit back his irritation. But he also didn't want to raise Finley's suspicions any more than they were already raised. She was adept at finding chinks in people's armors and exploiting them. Even his. "I announced I was leaving the company, as we discussed."

Finley smirked. "Is that what you call what happened in Embarcadero Plaza? An announcement?"

Of course, Finley had seen the story on the *Silicon Valley Weekly website*. Everyone in the Bay Area had seen it, judging by the text messages crowding his phone screen.

"Funny," Grayson growled. "If you're here to gossip, it'll have to wait. I have a job that requires my attention."

"So do I as your campaign manager, which means my job is gossip. Especially gossip about my candidate." The humor left Finley's expression and she leaned forward. "Who is she?"

It still hurt to recall how his sea goddess had left without a backward glance. "A guest at the ball. Obviously."

Finley gave him an assessing stare, then nodded. "As in obviously you don't know. And yet you were papped with her in a very public place." Finley handed Grayson her phone.

On the screen were two photos. The first was of Grayson and his companion before they unmasked. Her hands were cupping Grayson's face, and he was cradling her tight against him. They appeared oblivious to anyone else, wholly engrossed in each other. The intimacy of the photo took his breath away, like it had when he first saw the photo on his phone after his 5:00 a.m. workout.

But it was the other photo that caused him to regret his third espresso at breakfast as the acid rose in his stomach. In this image, he was clearly identifiable with his mask off, holding something white and silver in his hands and staring into the distance. The photo made him look resolute and strong. Amazing how the camera could lie. "Cinderella runs away from Silicon Valley's most eligible bachelor!" read the caption beneath it.

It took a concerted effort to keep his hand still as he handed the phone back to Finley. "Still don't know how the photographer knew it was me before I unmasked," he said, striving for nonchalance.

"Word to the wise for your next masquerade— Bitsy Christensen has most of the photographers in the Bay Area on speed dial. She probably had you followed to find out why you left her party early."

He shrugged. "Regardless, I've been kissing women for many years now. Some even publicly. It shouldn't be a surprise that while my last name is Monk, I don't behave like one."

"Leave the campaign slogans to me, please." Finley put the phone away. "But fine. Not knowing her name will make this more difficult, but not impossible."

Grayson opened his email. Three hundred and forty-two new messages stared back at him. At least half of them mentioned the gala in their subject line. "Spit it out, Finley. I speak four languages, but riddle isn't one of them. More difficult for what?"

"Setting her up as your campaign love interest."

Grayson blinked at his computer screen. "I'm sorry. I was reading my email and must have misheard you. Set who up as *what*?"

Finley sat on the edge of Grayson's desk and closed his laptop. "Focus, bro. Dad is going to announce his retirement soon. You have to be ready."

"Yeah, yeah, I know. What does that have to do with a—what did you call it? A love interest?"

"You're not married. You're not even dating someone seriously. Correct?"

"You know you are," Grayson growled. "So?"

Finley smirked. "So. It's a well-known fact the public loves a good romance. But they aren't so thrilled with a candidate who should be married by now—or at least in a serious relationship. It makes you seem like you can't commit. So why should they commit to you as their representative? Therefore, we need you to date someone. At least through the primary campaign. Hopefully until the general election."

Grayson stared at his sister. "I'm running for Congress. Not for *The Bachelor*."

"It's adorable you think there is a difference between the two—" Finley began.

Grayson stood up, intent on ushering Finley out of his office. This was ridiculous. And he didn't have time for ridiculous. Not ever, but especially not now.

"Wait, wait." Finley threw out her hands, palms up, in a placating gesture. "Please, sit back down."

Grayson remained standing. "You have five more minutes."

"Of course, there are differences between reality television series and running for office. But—" Finley held up her right index finger "—there are also similarities. Mostly in how the press shapes public perception. Sure, we'll put out policy papers, but take it from me. They don't generate clicks. However, a romance? And they're already calling her Cinderella? It's pure publicity gold. The story will dominate Facebook and Twitter." She took out her phone and held up the photos again. "And probably Instagram. You're disgustingly photogenic."

Grayson stared at his sister. "Please tell me you're still joking."

"Please tell me you aren't so naive." A hard light appeared in Finley's gaze. "I shouldn't have to remind you how important this election is to the Monk political legacy. You have the name. You look good on camera. And people like a self-made success story."

"Good. Then I don't need whatever it is you're proposing." Grayson sat down and reopened his laptop. Now he had 527 new emails.

Finley tried to close the screen again, but Grayson removed the computer from her reach. She folded her arms across her chest instead. "It won't be a slam dunk. An open congressional seat without an incumbent will receive a lot of interest from all corners. Barrett tasked me with getting you through the primary and onto the general ballot. This romance will help."

"Too bad I'll have to get by on hard work and addressing real issues instead." As he spoke, he received another twenty email alerts. His phone was set to silent, but the screen showed he had multiple missed calls. "Speaking of hard work, I need you to leave so I can get some done."

Finley shook her head. "The photos are blowing up on social media. We need to strike now, while the iron of public interest is hot."

Grayson stared her down. "Not going to happen. Even if I were to go along with your absurd plan, remember, I don't know her name." His chest twinged. Regret didn't get enough credit as a cause of cardiac pain. The pain sharpened when he remembered how the glow of passion in his mystery woman's gaze was replaced by horror as soon as she saw who he was. "Plus, you'd need to get her to consent to the scheme. That's even more unlikely."

Finley rolled her eyes, walked back to his sofa and sat, half leaning on the cushions. "It's a romance for your campaign. You date her, you dump her, you're done. She doesn't need to know anything more."

Grayson's hands hovered in midair over his keyboard. "What are you... I'm not going to lie—"

"Who said it's a lie? You'd still be dating her, wouldn't you?"

"I'd know it's a lie. No. That's final."

Finley turned her gaze to the ceiling. "Give me strength." Then she turned her withering stare on Grayson. "Look, I know Mom filled your head with all sorts of garbage about good relationships being 'until death do you part' and yeah, she did die before her marriage to Barrett had time to fall apart, so no wonder you think she's a great example. But for once in your adult life, could you act like an unenlightened Neanderthal, the way almost every other guy of my acquaintance does? Can't you casually date someone without needing to have a vision of wedding rings to dance in your head first?"

A knock caused both siblings to turn toward the door as Grayson's assistant poked his head into the room. "Sorry to interrupt, but I've been trying to call and text you without answer. You have a guest sent by Octavia Allen who insists on seeing you."

"Tell them to—" But his assistant was already swinging the door open wide.

And then *she* stepped over the threshold.

His sea goddess.

If his heart twinged before, now it stopped. Completely. Then started beating again, faster than if he had just finished a marathon. He blinked, once, twice, seven times to ensure he wasn't hallucinating. But he knew it was her. The silver-and-aqua ball gown had been replaced by black trousers and a silvery gray pullover sweater, and her chestnut hair fell in soft waves below her shoulders instead of being constrained in a braid. Her eyes were the same, however. Crystal blue, framed by sooty eyelashes and sharply angled brows.

"A guest?" he repeated, not daring to move in case she was a mirage after all.

His sea goddess stepped forward. "I apologize for showing up without an appointment, but Mrs. Allen sent me to speak to you without delay. I'm..." She stopped, and he could see her swallow. "I'm from Create4All," she finished.

"Create4All." His brain struggled to make sense of her words; he was still stuck on the impossibility of seeing her materialize in his office. Then reason clicked into place and he rose from his desk, his right hand extended to shake hers. "Right. Octavia's nonprofit. Kids and art."

"Yes." She accepted his handshake for the briefest of seconds, keeping her gaze focused on an invisible point somewhere beyond his left shoulder.

In his peripheral vision he could see Finley suddenly straighten up and pay attention, as if she were a starving puppy and the mystery woman was a bag of treats. That wouldn't do. Not while she was banging on about manufacturing a romance. He cleared his throat and injected what he hoped was the right amount of boredom into his voice. "This couldn't wait?"

That got his mermaid to look directly at him for the first time. "No. Mrs. Allen is aware we…met…at the gala." Her gaze flicked in Finley's direction. "She asked me to follow up—I mean, we were wondering if Create4All can count on your support. Despite…" She bit her lower lip. "Despite…everything?"

"Despite everything?" Finley tapped her right index finger on her chin. "What everything?"

A tantalizing pink filled his guest's cheeks. "Despite the announcement, I mean," she said after a beat. "About Mr. Monk stepping down from Monk Partners."

Grayson didn't like the sharpening glint in Finley's gaze. "I can give you fifteen minutes," he said to the woman, and then turned to his sister, his tone much firmer. "See you next week."

"Of course. I'm sure we'll have much more to talk about by then. I'll just close the door behind me, shall I?" Finley said blithely. Too blithe for Grayson's liking. She ushered his assistant out of the room, then turned to waggle her eyebrows at him. "Later, bro."

And with a soft click of the door, he was alone with his sea goddess. Again.

And there wasn't a clock tower anywhere within earshot about to chime and remind her to flee.

Nelle cleared her throat. Her heart pounded so hard that it was a miracle her whole body didn't shake, and her palms alternated between numb from cold and slippery hot from sweat. She did her best to keep her voice on an even keel. "Thank you so much for your time."

It was a very formal greeting, considering the last time she saw him their tongues were wrapped around each other. But in a way, this was her first meeting with Grayson Monk. And it came with the added pressure of knowing her job was on the line.

She had hoped their previous interaction would go unnoticed. They were outside the party, after all, not making out in front of everyone. But she still should have seen it coming. Anyone with a smartphone could be a paparazzo. Anyone with a social media account could cause a photo to go viral. Especially when one of the photo's subjects was a very photogenic billionaire.

Mrs. Allen made it clear she knew Nelle was the Cinderella. And she had known at the party it was Grayson in the Pierrot costume, thanks to being clued in by the gala chairperson. She had been thrilled to see Grayson motion Nelle over for a dance, which was why she told Nelle to join him.

She was not thrilled to see a photo of Create4All's new development director with her lips glued to a potential key donor. Although, she sniffed, she could look past it since technically it wasn't a breach of Create4All's policy. After all, Grayson was not affiliated with the organization—yet. But what Mrs. Allen could not, would not stand for was a Create4All employee who was so unprofessional as to publicly reject one of the wealthiest men in the Valley. A man who could potentially be the linchpin of their fund-raising goals for their five-year plan.

It took fast talking—very, very fast talking—but Nelle had managed to avoid being fired. And if Mrs. Allen ended the conversation believing the incident in Embarcadero Plaza was nothing but two old friends reconnecting and discovering sparks but wanting to keep their new relationship under wraps, only to have a minor spat caught on camera and blown up by the media, well, Nelle didn't disabuse her of the notion.

Unfortunately, Mrs. Allen also ended the conversation reiterating how much she was looking forward to receiving a very large donation from Grayson Monk in the near future. She didn't have to add, *or else*. Nelle received the message loud and clear.

She had to make that check happen. Not to keep her job, but so she could prove Mrs. Allen hadn't made a terrible mistake trusting Yoselin's judgment. For someone determined to avoid anything associated with the Monk family, things weren't working quite as Nelle had hoped. It had taken every ounce of willpower to force herself to follow her phone's navigation system to the Monk Partners office and not stay on the northbound freeway until she reached the Canadian border.

And now that she was in Grayson Monk's office, their gazes locked on each other, it took every ounce of willpower not to lose herself in memories of how his firm lips had coaxed hers to open to him, how his arms flexed and tightened around her. How the world had shrunk until it was just him, her and the sensual spell they wove together.

How she had run, so determined to leave him that she'd forgotten her mask. She was crushed when she realized she had abandoned the children's hard work on a city street.

He was even more attractive than she remembered. His crisp white shirt was open at the throat, revealing a triangle of tanned skin, his broad shoulders even more prominent without the baggy clown costume concealing them. His dark jeans fit as though specially tailored for him, sitting low on his narrow hips and outlining his thighs.

He cleared his throat and she jumped, just a little, heat saturating her cheeks at being caught cataloging his physique. His whiskey-brown gaze contained not a little heat of its own, and with a strange flutter in her chest she realized he had been engaged in his own perusal. She thanked whatever impulse had caused her to reach into the back of her closet to find her most flattering trousers this morning, still covered by a dry cleaning bag from before her move back to the West Coast.

"You're from Create4All?" he prompted. "Funny. The other night I would have guessed Atlantis."

Her cheeks were so hot she was amazed she didn't spontaneously combust on the spot. "Yes. I'm the interim development director. Mrs. Allen is…she thought we…that is, after seeing the photos…" Maybe he didn't know about the viral social media posts? "I mean—"

"I saw them, too," he said, as if reading her mind. "So. You're here because of Octavia. Or is there another reason?" His smirk said he had already decided what her answer would be, and it wasn't Mrs. Allen.

Damn it. The smirk should have made him appear smarmy and arrogant. But along with the glint of unholy humor in his gaze, it only made him devilishly appealing.

She cleared her throat and gave herself a firm mental shake. It was one thing to flirt with an appealing stranger at a masquerade ball as a test run for New Nelle, but she wasn't shielded by a mask now. Her gaze lifted to meet his straight on. "You're right. I'm here to apologize for leaving so abruptly the other night."

His eyebrows rose and he nodded. "Apology accepted. May I ask why?"

She took a deep breath. She had tried so hard to leave El Santo behind, first by running to New York City, then by inventing New Nelle. Only to be confronted with everything she tried to forget in the person of the man standing before her. It didn't help that she viscerally knew how his kisses could make her knees dissolve. And that her job depended on getting his signature on a hefty donation. "You can ask. And I do owe you an explanation. But I please ask that it won't affect any support you might give to Create4All." She straightened her spine, and then held out her right hand for another handshake. A real one. "An introduction should make it obvious. Hi, I'm Nelle."

He took her hand in his. This time she knew to brace herself for the electric jolt of his touch. "Nice to meet you, Nelle. I'm Grayson. But you know that."

"Nelle Lassen." She watched him closely, but his expression didn't change. "Doug Lassen's daughter."

She dropped his hand and looked down at the polished hardwood floor, not wanting to see contempt fill his eyes as he finally figured out who she was.

But the anticipated reaction did not come. Instead she heard, "I'm sorry. That name doesn't ring a bell."

She blinked. The Monk-Lassen feud had been a cornerstone of her formative years. "Doug Lassen? He went to school with your father? They started a law practice together after graduation?"

There was still no recognition in Grayson's gaze.

"The law practice disbanded before either of us was born," she said. "When your father ran in his first election." Her palms were wet from nerves, but she resisted the urge to wipe them on her trousers. "When your father set mine up to take the fall for misuse of client funds. My father was disbarred as a result."

And my family was destroyed.

Grayson's smirk disappeared. "That's a strong accusation."

Finally, the ground was solid under her feet. This was the reaction she expected to receive from a Monk. "It's not an accusation, it's the truth. So, I was shocked when I discovered it was you under the mask. I apologize for running, however. That was wrong of me."

His narrowed gaze searched her face.

She kept her chin high. "Please don't hold my identity against Create4All. The organization is doing amazing work—"

"You ran away because our fathers had some sort of falling out before either of us was born. Is that what you're trying to say?" He sat down on a deeply tufted leather sofa and indicated to her she should take the matching chair across from him. His long legs sprawled, and she remembered what they felt like through the flimsy layers of her skirt, warm and firm and solid—

She shook her head to clear it and remained standing. "I'm not trying to say anything. That *is* what happened. I also said Create4All is doing ama—"

"You ran even though that was a damned good kiss, if I do say so myself."

The searing heat climbed back into her cheeks, hot enough to start a brush fire. "It was…adequate. Anyway, Create4All makes a positive impact on young children and their parents. We're expanding our commitment to the community and building a new center—"

"Adequate?" He raised his eyebrows.

"As far as kisses go. But back to Create4All. We believe in purposeful play, which builds self-confidence and—"

"Pretty sure adequate is not the right word." He stretched his arms along the back of the sofa and leaned back. "Or maybe you aren't familiar with damned good kisses."

A smile played at the corners of his mouth. It made

her want to press her lips against his. To twine her arms around his neck as they crashed into each other, mouths open, their tongues competing to see who could coax the other to go deeper, harder, hotter. To show him just how spectacular she was at kisses that left her partner dazed and aching for more.

But.

He was a Monk. Trusting him would be like trusting a scorpion not to sting. She tore her gaze away from his and opened up her tote bag, taking out a colorful booklet. The cover featured photos of kids of all ages, genders and skin tones playing with clay, using computers to create illustrations and performing on stage.

"What I am familiar with is Create4All," she countered. Then, taking a deep breath, she launched into the speech she'd practiced a dozen times in the car before arriving at his office. "This is our prospectus. We've identified the perfect site for our new home. But to secure it, we need the guaranteed support of key sustaining donors like yourself. If you look at page twelve, you'll see where your money will be going. We believe in the strictest transparency—"

"I'll look at it." He took the glossy publication from her but didn't look at it. "I don't know what you think my father did to yours, or what stories you've been told, but—"

"Stories? Are you calling my dad a liar? He—" She slammed her lips shut. Standing up for what she believed in had already gotten her fired from one job. Antagonizing Grayson Monk further was a luxury she could ill afford. Not when her continued employment hinged on getting him to support Create4All. "I'm sorry, I didn't mean to—"

"No, I should apologize." He held his palms up in a placating gesture. "I wasn't saying—okay, it does sound that way. What I meant was everyone is the hero of his or her own story. That means someone else has to be the villain. I have no doubt your father is the hero of this story you're telling me. But this story doesn't have to be yours. After all, I'm not my father. And you're not your father."

He might not be Barrett Monk, but everyone knew it was a matter of time—a very short time—before Grayson would follow in his father's footsteps. "Technically, no, we're not. But blood is thicker than water. Isn't that how the saying goes?"

"Don't visit the sins of the father on the children," he retorted. "Whatever you think those sins may be."

And now he was back to insinuating she didn't know her own family history. "The apple doesn't fall far from the tree."

"In vino veritas," he replied.

"Chip off the old—wait. What?"

"In wine lies truth."

She narrowed her gaze. "Yes, I know what in vino veritas means. What I don't know is why you said it."

He put the prospectus down on the low coffee table in front of the sofa. "You're looking for sponsors, right?"

"Yes," she said slowly. She needed one sponsor in particular. Him.

He nodded. "And that's why you were at the masquerade. To meet people who can write large enough checks."

"It sounds so cynical when you put it that way," she said. "Create4All fulfills a vital need."

"Not saying it doesn't. But that's the bottom line. Correct?"

"If reduced to basics, yes."

He grinned. It warmed his expression, but there was a glint of wickedness that made her stomach flutter and tumble. "There's an event this weekend you should attend."

"Will you be there? If so, perhaps someone else should go. Mrs. Allen would be perfect." Despite her words, her heart started beating a little faster at the idea of seeing him again.

"I already turned down the invitation, but if you commit to being there, I'll bring you as my guest."

She regarded him for a beat, searching his gaze for any hint of an ulterior motive. "Why?"

He leaned forward. "Normally, I'd be happy to discuss a donation, but as you're aware I just resigned from the partnership. It's going to be a while before the new team starts making community development decisions. And my personal discretionary funds are… being held for another purpose at this time. I'm very sorry."

She took a deep breath, anticipating Mrs. Allen's reaction when she returned empty-handed. "I see. Perhaps we can set a future appointment—"

"However. If you're right and my father did commit nefarious deeds—" his mouth twisted to the side and she knew he didn't believe it for a second "—then I'd like to make up for it. This event will give you access to some of the heaviest hitters—and deepest pockets—on the West Coast."

He sounded sincere. But she knew well that sincerity could be faked. Knew it intimately. "But you said no to attending. I could go by myself."

"Not possible," he said, the glint in his gaze sharpening. "It's a drinks-and-dinner reception for an invitation-only summit of global CEOs. Very exclusive." He rose from the sofa and turned toward his desk, bending over to search through the papers on it. She couldn't help but notice how his dark jeans showed off one of the best examples of the male posterior it had ever been her privilege to see.

"You'll have plenty of opportunities for quality networking. And they're used to hearing pitches, so start practicing yours. It could use some polish." He wrote something down, then turned around and handed her a square of heavy card stock.

What the—her pitch was polished. She'd practiced it until her throat was sore. And to think she had been admiring his backside. She crossed her arms over her chest. "You cut me off before I could deliver it. Several times."

"Do you have experience pitching? To other people, not the mirror."

"Well, I…" No. She didn't. In her previous job, she did the writing. Other people delivered her words.

"You're not terrible. But I listen to pitches every

day, and so do most of the people you'll be meeting. Every second counts. You'll be judged and weighed from your first word." He indicated the card. "That's the invite. And that's my cell phone number. I'll send a car for you. Text me the address where it should pick you up."

"St. Isadore Vineyards," she read off the invite. Her eyebrows rose. "This is in Napa."

"It takes about two hours to get there from here depending on traffic, so plan accordingly." He seemed to read her mind again, because he followed that with, "Business casual. Nothing fancy. Definitely no costumes." He paused. "And no masks."

Her head jerked up. It sounded more like a challenge than a joke about their previous encounter. "I don't wear masks as a rule," she said. "Do you?"

Their gazes met, hers searching, his amused but assessing. "I don't like having my vision impeded," he finally said. "I rely on it too much."

Was he talking about how he saw her? If so, what did he see? She rubbed her thumb over the embossed letters on the card she was holding. If the people putting on the reception spent this much money on a throwaway invite… "You're sure I'll meet potential sponsors for Create4All?"

"Guaranteed."

She looked up from the invite to catch his gaze. "You're very free with other people's money."

"On the contrary. I'm very careful with other people's money. That's why they trust me with it. I know a good opportunity when I hear one, which is why I'm positive you'll find receptive ears."

She felt a spark of excitement starting to kindle. Bringing in heavy hitters as sponsors would go a long way to appeasing Mrs. Allen's anger over the Embarcadero Plaza photos. And if she brought in enough donations to secure the new building…then she didn't need to continue to court Grayson as a sponsor. She could make Mrs. Allen happy, secure her job and go back to her Monk-free life. She shook off the sharp twinge of disappointment at the thought. "You're sure?"

He closed half the distance between them. He was so near she caught his scent, reminiscent of fresh salt air mixed with pine needles crunching underfoot. It took her back to their kiss on the bench, her arms wrapped around his neck, his large hands cupping her rear end through thin layers of tulle that seemed to disappear beneath his touch. "If I weren't, I'd be a very bad investor. And I'm very good at two things. One—" his low bass voice rumbled in her ears "—is investing."

Her lips were dry. She wet them with her tongue. His gaze followed its path. "And the other?"

He came half a step closer. She was once again mesmerized by how his brown eyes were flecked with amber and ringed by dark mahogany. "Let's say negotiating. Although apparently not today. You haven't said yes."

Her traitorous body leaned, ever so slightly, in his direction. Any farther, and she would brush against his broad chest. She stared at the white expanse of his shirt, wondering if its fine cotton weave was as soft to the touch as it looked, wondering how he would react if she—she blinked. "I'm sorry. Yes to what?"

"To Napa." He paused. "Unless you'd like to dance. Again."

"Dance," she repeated, parting her lips and tilting her head without thinking. His dark gaze turned black, the radiating amber flecks in his irises becoming hard spots of light. If she raised her arms and drew him closer, she could bring his mouth down on hers, lose herself once more in the heat of his kiss.

A knock at the door, followed by the sound of it opening, caused Nelle to blink and jump, putting a few feet between her and Grayson as his words finally hit her. Dance. It was a reference to their conversation at the gala, nothing more. Her cheeks heated at how she'd almost made a fool of herself.

Grayson's assistant poked his head into the room. His expression was even more harried than when Nelle had first arrived at the offices. "Grayson, you have thirty-seven urgent phone calls, and I swear the servers will overload if you don't start clearing your email inbox. Also, your ten o'clock is here."

"Not how servers work, but I get the message. Tell Adam to start the meeting with Hassan. I'll be there when I can." After his assistant exited, Grayson turned back to Nelle. His voice became slower, rougher. "So. Napa. Or would you prefer dancing?"

"I'm keeping you from your work," she said, rushing her words to cut him off. She had done everything but issue Grayson Monk a command to kiss her. Him. Grayson. Son of Barrett. A Monk. What was it about him that ten minutes in his presence made her forget every lesson her father ever taught her? "Yes to Napa. Thank you for the offer of a driver. I'll text you my address."

Then she turned and escaped through the half-open office door, almost but not quite running as fast as she had the other night.

Coward.

But if she didn't leave, she was in danger of losing more than a mask.

Four

The drive to Napa from Fremont, where Nelle was staying with Yoselin until she had enough saved for an apartment deposit, was two hours as advertised— and an entire world away.

Perched on the smooth leather rear seat of the luxury town car Grayson had sent, true to his word, to pick her up, Nelle took in the landscape flashing past her. If the gala at the Ferry Building had been Oz, all bright colors and flashing lights, then Napa was Middle Earth. Green and gold hills in undulating waves stretched out as far as the eye could see in all directions. Rows of vines, lushly verdant and heavy with fruit, imposed linear order on the landscape. The sky was the crystal blue of her favorite sapphire earrings with only the occasional puffy clouds, perfectly marshmallow-like, to break up the azure expanse.

In short, the day was so ideal it seemed created by a computer to precise specification.

She could only hope the evening would continue to be as picture-perfect. Mrs. Allen had not been thrilled when Nelle returned from her visit to Grayson's office without a firm commitment from him to sponsor their new building, but the invitation to St. Isadore smoothed over most of her irritation. Nelle learned from her that the event was even more exclusive than Grayson had indicated. So exclusive that Mrs. Allen had never received an invite despite angling for one for years.

Getting on the guest list after only two months in the Bay Area certainly raised Nelle's status in the board director's eyes, but also heightened her expectations. And going as Grayson Monk's plus-one—Nelle's stomach squeezed as she refused to allow the word "date" to linger in her brain—didn't exactly erase Mrs. Allen's impression that Nelle and Grayson were involved beyond a professional capacity.

Nelle dropped her head into her hands. So much was riding on trusting a Monk. A Monk who claimed to be oblivious of their families' history. Sure, his kisses were hot enough to smelt copper and cause her usual good sense to burn away, but he had to know how his father won his first election. And he apparently didn't care. That was a waving red flag, on top of a flashing siren, blaring an eighty-decibel alarm.

But she couldn't deny she needed him. For Create-4All. Nothing more.

Or so she told herself.

The driver swung the car off the two-lane highway and onto a small, private road, allowing Nelle to catch her first sight of their destination. It took her breath away.

"I thought we were going to a winery," she said to the driver. The castle in front of her—there was no other word to describe it—did not look like a place of business. It belonged instead in France's Loire Valley, the chateau of a long-ago noble. Whitewashed stone walls soared into the sky, topped by a slate gray roof. Dozens of neatly arranged windows reflected the sunshine. There were even turrets. Turrets! And was that…? It was. A moat. "No way," she breathed.

"This is the address, ma'am." The driver crossed the bridge over the moat, which at closer glance might be more properly called a very large pond, and turned into a sweeping, curved drive. Pebbles crunched under the car's tires as he pulled to a stop in front of imposing wood doors that must have been two stories tall and nearly as wide. Box hedges, trimmed into strict geometric lines, flanked the entrance.

The driver came around the car and opened her door, extending his hand to help her out. Clutching her tote bag to her chest, she stared up at the mansion, not knowing what to do next. When she worked in finance, her boss had attended events at estates like this, but she had happily stayed behind at the office to do more research and craft more spreadsheets. The one experience she'd had with palatial estates came from a high school field trip to Hearst Castle. And then she'd had tour tickets and volunteer docents to tell her where to go.

"Do I ring the doorbell?" she asked, only to realize that while she was staring, the driver had returned to the car and was now pulling away.

Her first instinct was to take out her phone and order a shared ride service to take her home. But that was what the old Janelle would have done. New Nelle, on the other hand, took a deep breath and, squaring her shoulders, walked up the flagstone steps toward the door and raised her hand to knock. Then she hesitated. How did knocking work at a castle? Was there someone assigned to sit by the door in case a neighbor dropped by to borrow the lawnmower?

"Nelle!" The wind carried the sound from a distance. She had never been so glad to hear her name shouted before. She turned and saw Grayson, coming toward her in a walk-jog from the left side of the building.

He looked...amazing. There was no other word to describe him. The late-afternoon sun lit him from behind, outlining his broad shoulders and narrow hips as he strode toward her. He stopped in front of her and his left arm came up as if to pull her in for a hug. She found herself leaning forward to accept his embrace, until at the last second he dropped it into a handshake. "Hey," he said. "Glad you made it. Drive was okay?"

His stance was relaxed, his words sincere, and when his gaze met hers it spoke of nothing but pleasure at seeing her again. She liked that light in his eyes. She especially liked knowing she put it there. She—no.

Nelle shook a mental finger at herself. The Monk family was well known for their charm. *Don't fall for it.* She was here to secure her job. He'd offered to help. Nothing more.

Nothing, except for the deep tug of attraction she'd first felt at the gala and again in his office, and was now practically a gravitational pull. "The drive was great," she said with her best professional smile. "We arrived faster than I thought we would. Hope I'm not too early."

"Right on time," he said.

"And dressed okay? I have to admit I rather miss wearing a mask." She tucked a strand of hair that didn't need to be tucked behind her ear. Yoselin had picked out her outfit, a dark plum dress paired with knee-high black boots. Nelle thought she would be too self-conscious in a dress that clung to her curves, but the appreciation in his gaze made her very glad she had listened to her friend.

A smile lifted the left side of his mouth. "I was rooting for the bunny costume you mentioned, but this works very well."

"Thanks." She resisted the urge to return the compliment. This was his world. Of course he was perfectly attired for it. Instead, she glanced at the imposing doors. "I was about to knock."

He shook his head and held out his right arm,

elbow crooked. "The party is on the terrace. It's easier to take the side path."

She placed her hand on his arm, hoping he wouldn't notice the slight tremble in her fingers. Underneath her touch the finely woven wool of his sport coat was smooth, his flexed muscles firm.

Grayson led her down a stone path overhung with oak trees. It meandered along rows of grapevines, ending in a large flagstone terrace that wrapped the entire rear length of the castle. Nelle paused a moment to take in the view. It never ceased to amaze her how beautiful California could be, and Napa was one of its prettiest regions, rivaling landscapes painted by Impressionist masters. The air smelled of freshly cut grass mixed with wood smoke, coming from the massive cast-iron grill being prepared for the barbecue to come.

There were sixty, maybe seventy, people, arranged in small, animated groups. A few glanced up at Grayson and Nelle, their expressions welcoming. Still, beads of sweat dotted her hairline despite a welcome breeze. At the gala, she'd had Mrs. Allen and Yoselin nearby. Now…the only person she knew was Grayson.

She took a deep breath. This situation would have intimidated Janelle. But as Nelle, she threw her shoulders back, held her head high and—

The edge of her boot caught on an uneven flagstone, and she would have stumbled if it weren't for Grayson's steadying hand, immediately at her elbow. He glanced down at her. "Everything okay?"

She tried for a nonchalant laugh and then waved her hand, indicating the terrace before them. "What wouldn't be okay? So what's the plan? I mean, assuming you have a plan. Where do I start? Should I pick people to talk to, or will you bring them over to me, or should I wait until they come to me first, or—"

"Nelle."

She tore her gaze away from the crowd. "What?"

"Breathe in."

She did as he suggested, and it seemed to help. "Sorry. Just, I get nervous in front of big crowds."

"Give me your pitch." He dropped his arm in order to turn and face her. Her hand fell to her side, her fingers mourning the loss of the warmth radiating from beneath his sport coat and shirt.

"I'm sorry, you want me to pitch you? Now? But you've heard it. I don't—"

"Humor me. Create4All is..." He wagged his eyebrows in an invitation to complete the sentence, prompting a genuine laugh from her.

"Fine," she said and launched into her presentation. Yoselin had helped her to refine it, but she had to admit the video links Grayson texted her had been the most helpful. From them she learned she had fifteen, maybe thirty seconds to capture the other person's attention. Every syllable needed to count. As she delivered the pitch, she felt the knot of muscles holding her shoulders near her ears start to untangle. As no doubt had been his plan.

He nodded when she finished, and if she had stumbled over a word here or there under the intent warmth of his gaze, he didn't seem to notice. "That was good," he said. "You've got it down." His gaze fixed on a point over her right shoulder, and a grin appeared on his face. "Hey, Paco! Hassan!" He waved over two men, both dressed similarly to Grayson in khaki slacks, button-down shirts and sports jackets. "This is Nelle Lassen," he said to the newcomers. "She recently joined Create4All. Do you know it? It's like a start-up incubator but for kids. Helps them discover their creativity."

The taller of the two men extended his right hand to Nelle for a handshake, his dark gaze alight with interest. "Start-up incubator for kids. Intriguing."

"I can't take credit for that description, but I'm definitely stealing it from now on." She repeated the pitch she gave Grayson, her words increasing in confidence as the men listened and then started to ask questions.

Grayson remained by her side, so close that if she reached out her little finger, she would brush his thigh. As the conversation drew to a natural close, three more people joined their group and Nelle found herself pitching to them. Then others came over to be introduced. Throughout it all, she was acutely aware of Grayson. How he included her in the conversation even when the topic drifted away from Create4All and into the more esoteric ins and outs of buying and selling companies. How his body angled to ensure she was physically included in whatever group they were talking to. How he guided her wordlessly, seamlessly from one new arrival to the next with a light touch on her elbow.

As the sun sank in the sky, the last people to join their group drifted away. She rifled through the stack of newly acquired business cards in her right hand. CEOs, heads of international funds, global tycoons—more than a few of the names were commonly seen on the Forbes 400 list. It would have taken her weeks, if not months, of careful courting of assistants, lower-level executives and other gatekeepers to receive direct access to these people. An adrenaline high spiked her veins. "Pitching is fun."

"It is. Especially when you have a good product, which you do. I read up on Create4All."

"Oh? I thought you weren't interested in becoming a sponsor?" She continued to flip through the cards, making notes on each one for follow-up.

"I said I can't right now. I never said I wasn't interested." His voice lingered on the last word. She looked up, catching his gaze.

That was a mistake.

The setting sun lit his dark blond hair so it almost looked like a halo. The same rays warmed his gaze, turning his brown eyes to molten bronze. The effect reminded her of paintings she had seen in her art history class. Of a Renaissance prince, perhaps.

Then he smiled at her, slow and warm, and her breath caught.

Damn it. She didn't want to like him. She really didn't want to be this attracted to him, but the knowledge was ever-present of how his touch kindled sparks, how his kiss ignited sparks into flames. Her hands itched to reach out, run her fingers over his jaw, his cheek, pull his mouth down to hers to ensure he really was flesh and blood and not a painting come to life.

It was impossible to return to their old relationship: the one where she despised him on principle from a distance and he had no idea she existed. But maybe she could still extricate herself before the night went further. Before *she* went further. She cleared her throat. "So. Thank you for inviting me. I appreciate it. This is my first time working in nonprofit development and I don't have a network built up yet."

"It speaks well for you that you got the job anyway. Octavia Allen is very particular." The appreciation in his gaze was like a soft velvet blanket. She wanted to pull it tight around her, lose herself in its depths.

She looked away instead, focusing on the pink and purple clouds hovering above the hills. "It speaks well for my best friend who got me the job. I had to…let's just say finding a job in my previous career would have been difficult. Nor could I remain where I lived. She hired me because she knew I was in a bad place."

"Physically?" The question was light, but there was a hard note underneath.

She shook her head. "No. Emotionally. Although when your ego is torn to shreds and eaten by hyenas, it can feel like a brick hit you. Several bricks." She glanced at him from under her eyelashes. "Not something you're familiar with."

"Of course I am. Everyone is."

"Right." She smirked at him. "C'mon. You're Grayson Monk, the fair-haired golden boy. Barrett's heir apparent. You know full well all you have to do is snap your fingers and people scramble to give you what you want. Be honest. Have you ever had your ego trampled? Truly?"

His gaze narrowed. "I thought your problem was with my father. It sounds like your problem might be with me."

"My problem with you is your father, as we discussed." She bit her lower lip. She didn't expect Grayson to understand that while she didn't have a problem with him, personally—on the contrary, she was beginning to like him a little too much—she was very aware of the vast differences in their upbringings. "But…am I really that wrong?"

The sun disappeared below the horizon, and with it went its remaining heat. A cool wind replaced it, coming down from the hills and sweeping across the terrace. She resisted the urge to wrap her arms around herself, both to keep warm and to protect herself from the stillness creeping into Grayson's expression. She especially resisted the urge to lean into his warmth.

"No," he finally said. "You're not." Her head jerked up. He continued, "I've had a lot of help. My family name opened doors that were nailed shut to others. I've never had to worry about money or a place to sleep." His mouth twisted. "We just met, and you feel this way. I wonder if others share your perception."

"Why do you care? It shouldn't matter what I or anyone else thinks. Not to you."

His gaze searched hers. Then he nodded, as if he found what he was looking for. "It matters if I run for Congress."

She raised her eyebrows. "So the rumors are true? Barrett is stepping down and you're running for his seat?"

"Not officially. Not until he announces his retirement next month. And definitely not as far as the press is concerned." His tone carried a warning.

"I won't say anything. But still, why would you worry? You're a legend in El Santo. The entire county, for that matter. Homecoming king, nationally ranked swimmer in high school, now a titan of Silicon Valley. I'm surprised there isn't already a statue of you in Pioneer Park," she teased.

Too late, she realized she had said far too much. His gaze was laser-focused on her. She shivered, remembering their conversation in his office about masks and seeing beneath them. She would give anything to be safe behind a mask right now.

"Pioneer Park. You seem to be familiar with El Santo."

Busted. "I told you. Your father and mine were law partners. Where did you think that was?"

"My father started his law firm in Sacramento. El Santo became his home base during his first election."

She shook her head. "No, they practiced in El Santo. I grew up there."

"That's not—" He stopped, swinging his gaze to look over the grapevines. "The people of El Santo…"

he said, barely audible. He turned back to her. "That was you. At the gala."

"You know it was me at the gala. You took off my mask, remember?"

"During my speech. I overheard, 'the people of El Santo deserve better.' You were the speaker."

She was no longer cold. Searing heat flushed her cheeks, neck and chest. "I... I didn't mean for you to hear that... I'm so sorry...what I meant was—"

"Do you still feel that way after meeting me?"

She blinked several times. "I...no, of course not."

"You hesitated."

"No, I didn't—look, I know the voters love your father. They're bound to love you, too."

He would not let her off the hook. "I hear a *but* at the end of that sentence."

She took a deep breath. *Might as well be completely honest.* After all, it was her intention to never see him again after tonight anyway. Wasn't it? "But. Deep down, have you asked yourself what the people *deserve*? Will you be able to deliver it? Because, so far, your father hasn't." She held up a hand to stop the protest she saw forming on his lips. "I know, you probably think he's doing a great job. After all, he keeps getting elected. But El Santo needs a representative who cares about its people. I grew up on the east side of town near the train yards, overlooked and underserved. And I'm one of the lucky ones. I was able to leave El Santo for college and found work elsewhere. But what of the residents who are stuck with falling property values and no jobs to replace the ones that went offshore decades ago? What do you really know about life there? You've spent most of your time here, with them." She waved her hand in a sweeping motion to indicate the well-dressed men and women on the terrace. "I mean, why do you even want to run? Are you doing it because you want to, because it's the right thing? Or are you running because everyone just supposes you'll follow in your father's footsteps when he retires?"

He regarded her for a moment, his gaze dark and steady.

She cleared her throat. "Is the car nearby? I'll say my goodbyes now."

His brow furrowed. "Are you leaving?"

She blinked. "Well…after what I said…don't you want me to leave?"

Grayson remained silent, struggling to organize his thoughts. Four in particular flashed through his brain, quick as minnows and as slippery to catch.

The first was he should be happy she wanted to leave. The longer she stayed, the more likely someone would post a photo of the two of them on social media or let slip an inadvertent comment about how cozy he and Nelle appeared to be. And the next thing he'd know Finley would be in his ear babbling about "campaign romances" and "building a narrative for maximum voter identification."

His second thought was how beautiful she looked in the twilight. The red and amber streaks low on the horizon created gold highlights in her chestnut hair and threw into silhouette the curves outlined by her dress.

The third: he would be a damn fool to let her get away, now that he knew she was from El Santo. Finley and his father insisted Grayson's election was a foregone conclusion. They wanted him to spend his campaign funds on ads and messaging, not focus groups and polls. But Nelle was suggesting it wasn't as much of a slam dunk as his family was telling him. He needed straight talk, not smoke blown up his ass, if he wanted to fulfill his legacy of serving the public.

His fourth thought was wondering if kissing her would be even better with her hair down instead of in a braid. With her hair down, his fingers could slip through the silken strands—

Thought three it was. *Stay on thought three.* "No. Of course I don't expect you to leave," he said. "I appreciate your honesty."

She shrugged slightly and looked away. "You'd be one of the first. I haven't had the best reaction when I point out truths."

He smiled at her. "I'm not that fragile."

She half chuckled, half snorted. "No. That's not a word I'd apply to you. Still, I should leave, let you be with your friends."

"The invitation was for wine tasting and a dinner." He indicated the crowd starting to form at one end of the terrace around long tables laden with wine bottles. Waitstaff handed out empty crystal stemware. "And the wine tasting is about to start."

"I thought the invitation was to pitch your colleagues. And I do thank you for the opportunity." She set her jaw and squared her shoulders. "If you don't mind pointing me toward the car?"

He recognized determination when he saw it. Perhaps other tactics might work better. He indicated a stone staircase to their right. "The car will be waiting for you. Take these steps and they'll put you on the path to the front of the house and the driveway."

"Thank you again." She held out her right hand to shake and he took it. Her fingers squeezed against his, creating a chain reaction that made him wish he was wearing the baggy trousers of the other night. "I really do appreciate everything you've done to help me. Good night."

"Good night. I'll be sure to let Reid Begaye know he missed you." He let her hand go and began to walk to where the rest of the guests congregated.

It took a few seconds longer than he thought it would. "Reid Begaye?" she said from behind him.

Bingo. He fixed his expression before turning around. "He should be here later."

"Reid Begaye, as in the world's second richest man? The Reid Begaye who used to run Metricware?"

"He's the keynote speaker for the conference tomorrow morning. I was told he's running late because his foundation had a conflicting event this evening."

She nodded. "Right. That would be the foundation that gives away tens of millions of dollars each year to education nonprofits. Like Create4All."

"That's him. But since you want to go home—"

he shrugged with one shoulder "—I've heard your pitch. I'll give it to him if you want."

She crossed her arms over her chest and her right foot started to tap on the flagstones. "Something tells me you know he's on Mrs. Allen's short list of dream sponsors for Create4All. She might want to land him even more than she wants to land you."

"Octavia isn't subtle about what she wants. Reid will be sorry to hear you had to leave."

Her delectable lips pursed into the most kissable shape. Then she unfolded her arms and began to walk toward him, taking an empty glass off a passing waiter's tray. "I only like red wine," she said as she passed by, heading to join the rest of the guests.

Grayson followed her. He couldn't erase the grin on his face if the fate of the world depended on it.

Nelle strode through the crowd at the wine tasting, but once she passed Grayson, her head held high, she slowed her steps. The crisp businesslike tones that had filled the air in the late afternoon as men and women talked deals and strategies had given way to laughter and soft conversation as evening fell. Strings of small globe lights crisscrossed the terrace, casting a golden gleam that softened the rough stone patio and low walls. Catering staff walked among the tall cocktail tables draped with black cloths, lighting candles in cut-glass jars. Even the woodsmoke she'd detected earlier seemed to change, becoming heavier and sweeter as the time for grilling the vast amounts of meat and vegetables visible on the prep table drew nearer.

It was as if she had been transported from a business conference in Northern California to a dream vacation in Tuscany. Never in her wildest dreams would she ever believe she'd attend an event like this. Or meet the people whose cards were still clutched tight in her hand, much less Reid Begaye.

Janelle had been a caterpillar, she decided. Afraid to leave her leaf, unable to move very far or fast, her scope limited to what was immediately before her. But Nelle could be a butterfly. Able to fly above, travel far, range beyond the limits she had previously set for herself. She could dare believe those dreams would turn into reality.

Thanks to Grayson.

A year ago, she would have rejected the idea that her career success depended on a Monk. But when caterpillars morphed into butterflies, their perspectives changed, as well. Caterpillars' vision was limited to grains of dirt and individual blades of grass. Butterflies could see whole mountains and fields.

But what flew up must, of a necessity, come back down. The higher she went, the worse the inevitable fall would be. Did this sudden change in perspective make actual butterflies as dizzy as she felt now? Or did the dizziness have a different origin?

A light touch came at her elbow, and with it her answer. Grayson was the cause. She knew he stood at her side without turning her head. Knew it from the way the brush of his fingers against her sleeve put her nerves on immediate alert. Knew it from the way the atmosphere changed, both lightening her mood and darkening her desire to be near him.

"I have it on good authority the best table is to the far left," he said, his voice a deep rumble in her ear.

"And what makes it the best?"

"The owner of the vineyard is standing at it." He turned and waved at a group clustered around the table in question, who waved back at him.

"But of course, you know the owner." She allowed him to steer her toward the table, where she was quickly introduced to Evan Fletcher, who'd recently purchased St. Isadore Wines, and his business partner, Luke Dallas. Grayson handed her a stem of red wine before falling into a conversation with the other men about a possible new acquisition for Evan and Luke's company.

They included Nelle, but she was happy to let them catch up with each other without her. She drank deeply from her glass to avoid having to speak and reveal just how much she wasn't paying attention. But mostly she downed the wine so she would have an excuse to keep her hands busy, so she wasn't tempted to cling to Grayson's arm, to twine her fingers with his.

Maybe Grayson was right. Maybe the past was precisely that: the past. There was no reason why it should impact the present, much less the future. The previous generation's actions didn't have to dictate her view of the current one.

Did it?

Her thoughts chased each other, bouncing and skittering inside her skull. Before she knew it, her glass was empty. Oops. Weren't people supposed to sip and then spit out the wine when at a tasting? Or at least that was what the internet said.

She looked up to see Evan watching her with raised eyebrows. "I like a healthy appreciation," he said. "Here, let me top off your glass. I'm not sure you got the entire sensory experience with such a small sip."

Usually the suggestion she had made a social faux pas, no matter how slight, would be enough to send her shrinking into the shadows until she could back out via the nearest exit. But Evan's tone was light and teasing, Luke's smile was friendly and welcoming, and Grayson's gaze—Grayson's gaze made her lungs lose all sense of rhythm. Her breathing stopped, then sped up, then stopped again.

She held out her glass and searched her memory for phrases she read while researching what to expect at a wine tasting. "Full-bodied, nicely acidic with a touch of sweetness for balance, and pleasantly dry. In other words, fill 'er up." She tapped the brim. "To here."

"Ha!" Evan did as she requested, and then gave her an unopened bottle. "Here. Take this home. You earned it." He then turned to Grayson. "I like her," he said.

Nelle's gaze met Grayson's. If the intense light in his eyes caused her breathing to be erratic, now it caused her heart to beat three times faster than usual. He continued to hold her gaze as he answered Evan. "Me, too."

She sipped her wine slowly this time, very aware that her cheeks must be the exact same shade of crimson as her beverage. But the warmth in her cheeks was nothing compared to the heat building deep inside. A heat that only grew hotter when their arms brushed. If she had wondered if Grayson thought of this as a mere business excursion, she now had her answer.

This was a date.

And she was not unhappy about it.

Five

Grayson watched Nelle as Luke drew her into a conversation about child development and Create4All's recommended best practices. She laughed, throwing back her head, exposing the long pale expanse of her neck. He wanted to press his lips there. Taste her. Kiss a path from where a gold locket snuggled in the hollow of her throat to the curve of her jaw, follow it around to where that dimple teased him by appearing and disappearing as he watched. The kiss in Embarcadero Plaza would always be seared on his brain, but it wasn't enough. He craved more.

Evan clapped him on his shoulder and he reluctantly dragged his focus away from her. He and Evan had met at a similar function to this one, albeit when their bank balances were much closer to zero. Grayson had invested in two of Evan's previous start-ups, which performed well if not spectacularly, before coming up with the brainstorm to partner him with Luke Dallas. Together, their combined talents and complementary skills had created a medical technology company that rocketed straight from the gate into the stratosphere. And that had allowed Evan to buy St. Isadore.

Grayson lifted his glass. "This is good. I'm not usually a fan of blends."

"It's something the head vintner came up with. Only a few bottles are ready for drinking."

"He has a hit on his hands." Grayson finished his glass.

Evan watched the crowd gathered around his director of operations, who was leading them through a structured wine tasting. "You mean, she has a hit on her hands. Yeah, I know, she's told me."

Grayson raised his eyebrows at the coolness in Evan's tone. "Where is she? I'd love to meet her."

Evan's distant gaze snapped to Grayson's. "Working," he said, his consonants precise. "Or at home, since the workday is over. Or doing a thousand other things. How would I know?"

"I see." Grayson smiled as he poured himself another glass. Evan's speech only became clipped like that when something—or someone—had burrowed under his skin and continued to prickle.

"Speaking of seeing." Evan put his wineglass down, the better to lean his forearms on the table.

"I wasn't expecting to see you. You said you weren't attending this year's summit."

Grayson shrugged. "Changed my mind."

"You don't do that. Not as a rule." Evan glanced at Nelle. "I don't have to be psychic to know why, though."

"If you were psychic, you'd know where your head vintner is."

"Ha, ha," Evan deadpanned. "Nelle is the woman from the gala, right? And the photos in *Silicon Valley Weekly*."

Grayson started to answer, but Nelle caught his gaze and smiled. A wide, open, gorgeous smile. Her eyes shone, reflecting the glow of the candles and the strings of lights above. She raised her glass of wine to him and then turned back to her conversation.

"Yeah," Evan said, his tone dryer than a California drought, "she's the one."

"What's that supposed to mean?" Grayson's brows drew together. He didn't have many close friends. Oh, he had acquaintances and colleagues enough to fill several college football stadiums. But good friends? The kind who would be there at 3:00 a.m. to bail him out of jail, no questions asked? He could count those on the fingers of one hand. And he was about to lose one of those if Evan didn't explain himself.

Evan raised his hands in a conciliatory gesture. "It's bad enough I have to deal with Luke swooning over his wife on a daily basis at work. Now when we hang out, I'll have to listen to you wax poetic about true love. I won't be able to escape."

True love? Grayson glanced at Nelle, who was still

intent on her discussion with Luke. His gaze traced the graceful contours of her face, the generous curve of her chest above her hourglass waist.

He liked her. He hoped he could persuade her to share her perceptions of El Santo and what the people of the district needed. And yes. He wanted her.

But like wasn't love. Lust definitely wasn't love.

Love wasn't on the schedule. He had a month to wind down his obligations to Monk Partners before he would be required to stand by his father's side as Barrett announced he wouldn't be seeking reelection. And then Grayson's campaign would begin in earnest.

He took his family's legacy seriously, and his responsibilities even more so. He had no time right now to discover if the electricity that arced between him and Nelle was a harbinger of deeper emotion or merely his libido demanding to get its way.

And he certainly wasn't going to enlist her in Finley's ridiculous plan. He would not use her as a prop, much less expose her to his sister's single-minded tactics. He really did like her.

Grayson tuned back in to hear Evan sigh. "Next thing I'll know, boys' night will be pizza for one and games of solitaire instead of Cuban cigars and hands of poker."

Grayson side-eyed him. "When have we held a boys' night? Or played poker?"

"It's metaphorical." Evan reached for the nearest open wine bottle.

Grayson took the bottle from Evan's grasp and moved it to the other side of the table, where it joined several empty ones. "I'm beginning to think a vine-yard might not have been your wisest choice of in-vestment."

"Remember how Luke looked at Danica the night of last year's Peninsula Society gala? I see the same thing in your eyes, my friend."

"I think you've seen the bottom of your glass too many times. Please tell me you're staying here tonight and not driving back to the city."

Evan laughed. "I'm as sober as a judge presiding over a patent theft trial." He indicated the guests mi-grating toward the tables of freshly prepared food. The night breeze carried the scent of well-seasoned steak and grilled vegetables, and plates were already being heaped high with food. "Dinner's on. But the real question is, have you decided on what—or who—you're having for dessert?" He wagged his eyebrows and clapped Grayson on the back. "I've got to mingle and sell a couple of bottles of wine to help pay for this thing. Talk to you later."

"Not if I can help it," Grayson muttered into his glass.

"What was that?" Nelle appeared at his side, Luke having left to join Evan in the crowd around the bar-becue pit. She was so close he could reach out an arm, encircle her waist and pull her against him. He reached out his hand—

And motioned at the open bottle, still about half full. "I was saying I never leave good wine behind if I can help it. Want another glass?"

He was stalling, he knew. They should join the others eating dinner. But the sooner they ate, the sooner the end of the night would come. And the sooner he would have to say goodbye to her.

She glanced at the line for the food, then back at the bottle, and held out her glass. "I don't think I tried this one."

He poured a small amount in it, then glanced at the label. "This is a Cabernet Sauvignon blend. According to the tasting notes—" he picked up a sheet of paper dotted with ring-shaped stains and tried to read it in the dim light "—you should detect notes of plum, cherry and black currants."

She took a sip, considered for a minute, and gave him a half smile, half grimace. "Can I make a confession? I just taste wine."

He laughed. "Me, too. But we didn't go through the ritual wine tasting steps."

"Trust fancy people to make wine more complicated than it needs to be. You pour, you drink. What more needs to happen?" She reached across him to take the bottle and top off her glass. Her scent wafted over him, a light jasmine note that reminded him of spring and fresh beginnings. He remembered how it had filled his senses as her mouth crushed against his, his hands running over the hard peaks of her breasts—

Damn it. He was already responding to her. He cleared his throat. "Several things happen. For example, at a tasting you consider the wine's…" He dropped his gaze so he wouldn't be mesmerized by how the skin above the deep V of her neckline gleamed in contrast to the velvet of her dress. But when he looked down, he was greeted by the sight of knee-high boots, their supple black leather hugging beautifully shaped calves. "The wine's, um, legs."

She raised her eyebrows. "Wine has legs?"

"Some varietals do, depending on age. And then there's the—" He made the mistake of glancing up as Nelle drank deeply, her eyes closed in appreciation, her lips wet on the glass "—mouthfeel."

She threw him a glance from under her lashes. "My mouth feels like I just drank wine."

He would give anything to discover for himself how her mouth felt, right that very second. He put his hands in his trouser pockets and rocked back, hoping the tightness beginning to make itself known in the fabric wouldn't be apparent to her. "To properly assess mouthfeel, you hold the wine in your mouth."

Her right hand hovered in midair, the glass halfway to her lips. "Hold it in my mouth?"

He nodded. "To get the feel."

She put her wine glass down and slowly turned so they stood face-to-face. Barely a hand's width separated them. "And after I've held it in my mouth?"

He reached for the bottle of wine standing at her elbow. It was either drink more or grab her hand, break into the winery, and find a secluded room in which to show her just what, exactly, should happen next. She reached for the bottle at the same time. Their fingers met, collided. Neither let go.

"You have a choice." His voice was raspy. He tried to work more moisture into his mouth.

"Do I swallow?" Her thumb moved where it met his, grazing over his skin, so slightly that he wondered if he were imagining it.

"That's a possibility. Although…" He paused. No, her thumb was definitely brushing against his. "Not recommended."

Her pink tongue darted out to wet her lips. He followed its path with his gaze. "Really. I would think differently. Otherwise, it's such a waste. Of wine."

"Not if there are hours—of wine tasting—to come." He leaned down, his mouth almost at her ear. "If you drink too much, there's a risk of finishing early."

Her lips curved upward in a slightly wicked smile. "I don't want that. The one thing I do know…about wine…is a lingering finish is preferred." Her fingers were now enmeshed with his where they held the bottle together.

At the gala she had appeared as a sea goddess, regal, almost unapproachable. Now, with her chestnut hair down and blowing in the breeze, her eyes dark and glittering in the glow of the string lights above, her lips stained red with wine—now she was unmistakably human, lusciously curvy flesh and blood. His hands ached to push aside the wide V of her neckline, exposing more bare skin for his mouth to worship. To free those glorious breasts that filled his hands in his dreams every night. He wanted to see if he could coax that dimple to appear by whispering what he wanted to do with her, here, now, despite the crowd gathered on the other end of the terrace.

The wind shifted, bringing with it the smell of mesquite smoke and tri-tip. He held her gaze with his. "Are you hungry?"

She audibly inhaled. "Depends. For what?"

He smiled at the echo of her words from the gala, his fingers remaining locked with hers. "There's a barbecue over there. Or…"

"Or?" She breathed the word.

"Grayson! There you are!"

With an oath, he dropped his hand from hers and turned to see who was hailing him. A man, wearing his signature Stetson along with his sport coat and khakis, waved at him from across the terrace. Of course. He always did have perfect timing.

Nelle turned her head to follow his gaze. "Who is that?"

"Who else? Reid Begaye has arrived."

Nelle didn't know whether to laugh with relief or cry with frustration as she watched Reid Begaye weave his way through the clusters of people, shaking hands and exchanging words, but staying on a clear beeline to where she and Grayson stood. If Reid had put off his entrance for even a minute longer, she had no doubt she and Grayson would already be in his car, driving through the night to the first place with an accommodating bed. In fact, with the way her legs still trembled and her breathing still stuttered, they might not have made it to the car, instead breaking into the winery's main building to find a secluded room.

Thank goodness for wealthy philanthropists who

weren't named Monk, or she might have done something she would regret in the morning. And no, it wouldn't have just involved a forced entry.

She stepped away from Grayson, putting the bottle back down on the table. She also put a good foot of distance between them. A few deep, steadying breaths and she was ready to give Reid her most welcoming smile as he shook hands with Grayson.

"I hear you're looking for me," Reid said to Grayson, before extending his right hand to her. "Hi. Reid Begaye."

"Nelle Lassen," she responded. "It's a pleasure to meet you."

Reid was tall, about the same height as Grayson, but that was where the comparison stopped. Grayson was lean, his swimmer's shoulders lending the only appearance of bulk. Reid was well muscled, his sports jacket obviously custom-tailored to contain his broad chest and beefy forearms. Grayson's dark blond hair always looked as if he had just come from the beach, while Reid's was precisely cut without a hair out of place. Grayson's expression was generally open and friendly, as if he'd heard a good joke and couldn't wait to share it, while Reid's was opaque without a hint at his thoughts. It didn't help that his hat kept most of his face in shadow.

Still, she found herself liking him. His handshake was firm and no-nonsense, his gaze direct, and she began to relax despite everything she had at stake.

"So you're Nelle," Reid responded. "I thought so, seeing as you're here with him." He jerked a thumb at Grayson. "Luke Dallas said we should speak. You have a children's charity?"

"I work for one. Create4All. I'd love to tell you more about it."

Reid smiled. It changed his face, lighting it from within. Nelle hadn't thought of him as particularly handsome before, more interesting-looking than conventionally attractive, but now she changed her mind. It must have shown, as Grayson closed the space between them, angling his shoulder so he stood between her and Reid.

She bit back a smile, only to find Reid examining her more closely. "Tell you what," he said, turning his back so as to cut Grayson out of the conversation, "it's been a long day for me. I flew in from Sydney and went straight to an event and then came here. I can't tell my right hand from my left hand. I'm only here to talk to folks like this one—" he jerked his thumb at Grayson "—and for them I don't need a working brain."

"Don't need a working brain? That explains why you made the deal at last year's conference to sell Swynn Industries when I advised against it," Grayson said with a smile. "And the buyers ran it into the ground and declared bankruptcy, like I told you they would."

Reid shrugged, his gaze still locked onto Nelle's. "Fine, Grayson was right. Once. Let's allow him to enjoy it while it lasts."

Nelle laughed. "I hope he's right about your support of children's causes."

"That makes twice he's right." Reid turned and clapped Grayson on the shoulder. "So. Were you asking around for me just to rub my nose in a bad deal?"

Grayson shook his head. "No. Nelle is the one looking for a deal this year."

Reid nodded. "Ah. Got it." He turned back to Nelle. "As I was saying, I can wheel and deal with guys like this while I'm three-quarters asleep, but I like to be fully awake when discussing my foundation. Let's have breakfast tomorrow before my keynote and you can tell me about your organization. Seven thirty okay? Conference hotel restaurant. I already have a reservation, but I'll cancel the existing meeting and put you in instead."

"She'll be there," Grayson said before she could respond. "Thanks for this, Reid. I know your schedule is tight. You're off to Asia after this, right?"

Reid's mouth twisted. "Yeah. Well, business—and good causes—stop for no man, even if life has another plan in mind." He clapped Grayson on the shoulder again. "Good to see you, even if it only reminded me of my lapse in judgment." Then he took Nelle's hand in his. "And very good to meet you. See you tomorrow."

He left almost as suddenly as he arrived, swallowed by another group of people who had obviously been waiting for him to join them. Nelle turned to Grayson. "Seven thirty a.m.?"

"It's your one chance to speak with him. He's currently embroiled in a fight for control of his family's assets—it's a long story. You must have impressed him to get on his schedule." His jaw tightened.

"You did the impressing. He's meeting me because of you," she pointed out.

"He doesn't do favors for just anyone. He liked you." A tiny muscle started to jump in his jaw.

"Is the car nearby? If I want to get any rest before the meeting, I should have left here hours ago." She'd need to wake up at 3:00 a.m. to get herself looking presentable and arrive on time in spite of any traffic snarls she might face. Better set her phone alarm while she was thinking of it. The last thing she wanted was to sleep through—

"Oh no."

"What's wrong?"

She showed him the news alert on her phone screen. "A brush fire broke out to the south of us a few hours ago" She clicked on the story and started to read. "It doesn't sound too bad…no homes are in its path… Oh, wait, here's an update." She read it and then looked up to catch Grayson's gaze, feeling sick to her stomach. "Smoke is drifting over the freeway and threatening drivers' visibility. The highway patrol is closing all lanes as a precaution."

"May I see?"

She handed him her phone and squeezed her eyes shut, trying to think of an alternative way to get home. There were other freeways between Napa and the East Bay, but it would mean taking a much more circuitous route. She'd have barely enough time to grab a vat of coffee to go and a change of clothes before needing to turn around and head back.

"It sounds like it will be contained by morning." Grayson handed the phone back to her. "Freeway should be open by then."

"That's good," she said. "Although it's going to take forever to get home tonight." The wine in her stomach sloshed in a very unappetizing manner. "I'm glad I came, and it was very nice of you to invite me, but I really should get going now and—"

"Nelle." It was one syllable, but it was warm and kind and understanding. "Breathe."

"It's just…did you know the Begaye Foundation gave ten million dollars to an organization similar to Create4All in Chicago? Granted, the Chicago non-profit is much larger, but if I can convince him to give even one tenth of that to us, it will mean our capital budget will be secure and we can go ahead with the new site. I can't screw this up."

"You won't."

She tried to smile. It was wobbly. "Can you say goodbye to Luke and Evan for me? And could the driver stop at a fast food drive-through on the way back?" She was going to miss dinner. "And, um, I know I'm forgetting something…"

Grayson considered her for a minute. Then he took out his phone, punched in a few numbers, and started to speak. "Hi, it's Grayson Monk. Can you add another room to my reservation for tonight?"

She whipped her head around to stare at him. He held her gaze as he continued speaking. "Thanks.

Would you transfer me to the hotel's boutique?" He listened for a minute, then spoke again. "Hi. Did the front desk—great. I'm going to put a friend of mine on the phone. Send everything she asks for to my room and put it on my account."

He held out his phone to Nelle. "One solution is to stay at the conference hotel. There's a room available and I've got the hotel's shop on the line. They carry a wide range of clothes and toiletries. Order what you need for tonight and tomorrow." At her openmouthed surprise, he added, "On me. I insist."

She stared at him. So many conflicting thoughts and emotions jockeyed for attention that she couldn't sort through them all. She finally settled on, "I can't accept."

"You're in this situation because of me. It's the least I can do."

"I don't…" She shook her head, hoping to clear it. It only scrambled her brain more. On the one hand, it would make her life infinitely easier if she stayed at the same hotel where her breakfast meeting was taking place. On the other, it would put her even deeper in Grayson's debt. Yes, so far he'd followed through with everything he promised, not a hint of double-dealing in any of his actions. But he was still a Monk.

And someone she found very, very, *very* attractive. It was one thing to heavily flirt over wine. It would be another to know they were sharing a roof, albeit in a hotel with numerous rooms. "I'm not sure—"

He held the phone to his ear. "Are you still there? Sorry to keep you on hold… Great. Send a selection of women's clothes in size...?" He raised his eyebrows at Nelle.

She folded her arms across her chest. "I'm not telling you my size."

"Let's say in an eight," he said into the phone. "Business casual. Plus anything else one might need for an overnight stay—yeah. Send some of those, too. Thank—"

She took the phone from him. "Size twelve," she said to the boutique employee on the other end, then handed it back to him. He finished the conversation and then had the audacity to grin at her.

"I still haven't said yes," she reminded him.

"But now you have a choice," he said. "If you want to leave, I'll have my driver take you home via the safest route possible. If you would like to stay—" his crooked grin deepened "—you can have a dinner prepared by a Michelin-starred chef and a good night's rest. Up to you." He shrugged.

Nelle pressed her lips into a thin line. It would serve him right if she called his bluff and asked for the car... Oh, who was she kidding? She was the person bluffing. There was only one good choice. Yes, he made the choice possible, but that didn't mean she had to shoot herself in the foot and not accept. "I'm paying you back for the room and clothes," she said. He opened his mouth, but she cut him off. "That's nonnegotiable."

Their gazes engaged in a slight skirmish before he relented, extending his arm to her with its elbow bent. "As you wish. Meanwhile, the line for the buffet is now nonexistent. Shall we?"

She found her hand resting on his bicep before she could form a conscious thought. The now familiar electricity sparked anew. "Lead on."

She might as well enjoy his company for the rest of the evening before she said good-night to him—and goodbye. They would have separate rooms at the hotel. She could meet with Reid Begaye and then leave. She could even rent a car to drive home and not have to bother him again.

Ever.

Her heart constricted into a tight, painful knot at the thought.

Six

Nelle did not, as it turned out, have a separate room.

She stared at the hotel front desk clerk, her lower jaw somewhere between her knees and her ankles. "Could you repeat that?"

The clerk's gaze was wide with apology. "I am very sorry. The hotel is sold out. Between the conference and the guests who decided to stay an extra night thanks to the brush fire, I'm afraid there are no rooms left."

"But I called," Grayson interjected.

Nelle glanced at him. Their easy, flirtatious camaraderie had continued for the rest of their time at the winery. But when they got into the car for the ride to the hotel, they'd pulled away from each other to check their phones for messages and emails. Nelle quickly dealt with hers—Mrs. Allen wanting a recap of Nelle's evening, Yoselin wanting one, as well, but with an emphasis on activities featuring Grayson—but Grayson dove headfirst into his phone with a crease forming between his brows and didn't resurface until the car pulled up in front of the hotel's main entrance. The crease was still there.

The hotel clerk typed on his computer. "Yes, Mr. Monk, I see that in your file. You asked for another room. So we upgraded you from a suite to a bungalow. There is separate living and dining space in addition to the usual sitting area found in our suites."

"I made it clear I wanted an additional hotel room. Not extra space." Grayson's words held the snap of a steel trap springing closed.

The clerk took a whole step back. "We're very sorry for the misunderstanding. The upgrade is, of course, complimentary, but we cannot accommodate a room change."

Grayson raised an eyebrow.

The clerk's Adam's apple bobbed. "I can try our sister hotel, if you like?"

"Your manager, please. I'll wait." Grayson had his head turned away from her, but Nelle still saw tight muscles in his jaw jump while the crease in his forehead grew deeper. She touched him on the arm to get his attention.

"It's okay," she said. "The bungalow sounds like it's more than big enough for the two of us. It's still a better plan than trying to get home while the freeway is closed."

He finally turned to look at her, anger and apology present in equal measures in his expression. "I want you to be comfortable. If I can't resolve this with the manager, I'll stay here in the lobby. You can have the room."

"It's not a room, it's a bungalow. Don't be a martyr. Especially not on my account." She turned back to the clerk, who was trying desperately to look like he wasn't eavesdropping. "We'll take it."

The clerk said a few words into his headset, then smiled at Grayson. "If you would wait here, I'll have one of the staff escort you to where you're staying. We've already taken your bags from your car, Mr. Monk, and put them in the bungalow."

Under any other circumstance, Nelle would have been thrilled and amazed to find herself staying at the Auberge de la Lune. Even she knew it was one of the most exclusive hotels in the country, if not the world. And in a bungalow! Separate from the rest of the hotel, set back amongst tall trees and completely private from prying eyes, the cabin-like space was everything she could have known to imagine and then more. It was like stepping into one of her favorite Instagram accounts come to life, and she mentally cataloged the two rooms and their accompanying bathrooms to describe them to Yoselin later.

The smaller of the rooms held the bed, made up with crisp white linens, plush silver gray blankets, and plump, down-filled pillows. Nelle poked her head in and out, intending for Grayson to make use of it. The larger room was the living space, divided into distinct areas. A small kitchenette occupied one corner, next to a wet bar stocked with bottles from brands Nelle had only ever seen on the very top shelf at pricey bars. The refrigerator was stocked with various luxury snack foods, and its lower half was specially designed to store wine. She recognized labels from nearby wineries.

Blond hardwood furniture gleamed everywhere, tempting her to touch the expensive but inviting surfaces. There was a desk with a conference table extension along a second wall, while a square fireplace cut seamlessly out of the far wall was the focal point of the space. The gas logs were alight, throwing dancing shadows on the wide, overstuffed sofa, two easy chairs and a sheepskin rug placed in front of the fire. She peeked inside a sizable closet and found additional pillows and throw blankets.

But her gasp was reserved for the items on display on the various tables dotted around the room. On the console that stretched the length of the back of the sofa was an ice bucket containing a bottle of champagne and a bottle of white wine. A bottle of red wine, chocolate-dipped strawberries and a box of handmade milk chocolate truffles accompanied it. One table to the side of the sofa held a selection of mineral waters in various flavors and a basket of artfully arranged fruit. And on the other side table were several shopping bags bearing the name of the hotel's boutique.

She heard Grayson come up behind her. "What, no rose petals?" she joked, indicating the champagne. At least she thought she was joking. "The strawberries are a nice touch, though."

Grayson picked up a small folded card from where it was halfway hidden by the chocolates. "It's from the hotel's management. A small token of their apology for the mix-up." He let the card drop back onto the table and made a beeline for his luggage. He opened up the smaller of the two cases and took out a laptop, then settled at the desk.

She grabbed a water, keeping her gaze off the romantic display of fruit and wine. "I like the way they apologize. What's in the shopping bags?"

For the first time since they arrived at the hotel, a smile creased his face. "Your things for tomorrow."

She peeked inside the first bag. Fine wool trousers in various shades of gray, black and cream were nestled in sheets of tissue paper next to sweaters so soft they must be pure cashmere. The second bag contained makeup and basic skin care necessities, by a brand she knew from its mention by celebrities on beauty websites. And the third—searing heat rose in her cheeks and she was amazed she didn't set the place ablaze by proximity. It held silky scraps of lace tied with ribbons, so impossibly delicate they could only be called lingerie. They were the furthest things possible from her usual cotton underwear.

She looked up, hoping he would put the color in her face down to the nearby fire. "I'm sure something here will work. The boutique will take back the rest?"

"Of course."

She gathered the bags up. "Do you want me to wait until you finish your work before I make up the sofa?"

He looked up, his gaze distant. "Why would you do that?"

"Why would I wait for you to finish your work?"

"Make up the sofa." He nodded at the door to the bedroom. "That's where you're sleeping. I'm fine with the sofa as it is."

"I can't let you sleep out here. Have you seen that bed? It looks amazing—" She stopped, her thoughts going to earlier that night and her desperate desire to find a room, any room where they could slake the desire that seemed to always overtake them. She cleared her throat. "I mean, I'm infringing on you already. You take it."

He turned back to the desk, his back straight, his shoulders set. "I have work that can't wait. If I were alone, I'd be out here anyway. The bedroom is yours." His tone suggested he wouldn't discuss it further.

"If you're sure." She clutched the bags to her chest, not sure what to do next. Should she give him a hug goodnight? Or a kiss—a chaste one, to thank him for the evening? Or—

"Sleep well," he said, his gaze locked on his screen. "If I don't see you in the morning, best of luck with your meeting. The car will be waiting for you when you're done."

He was dismissing her. She should be glad. This was what she wanted, a clean farewell with no hint of seeing each other again. So why did her hands shake and her eyes sting? She cleared her throat and put a cheery smile on her face.

"Sounds good. Good night," she replied, and closed the bedroom door behind her. Through it she heard him moving around the other room, typing on his keyboard. She sighed. So much for engaging in a session with her right hand, starring him in her fantasies. She'd have to find another way to lull herself to slumber despite knowing he was just a few feet away.

Several hours later, she was still wide awake.

She should be able to sleep. The bed was one of the most comfortable she had ever lain on. Firm but enveloping. Like a cloud, but with perfect support. The linens were crisp and cool and slid across her skin with a silken whisper. She had her choice of pillows, from ridiculously overstuffed goose down to memory foam that contoured to her head and neck. The room was dark, the blackout curtains shutting out not only light but apparently sound from outside the bungalow. There was nothing to disturb her slumber.

Nothing, except her knowledge of who was on the other side of the bedroom door.

She scowled and punched a pillow back to its perfect shape. She was dehydrated. That must be it. After an evening of wine and barbecue, she required additional water. She turned on a light. The room was as she remembered. No mini bar, as the bungalow had its own kitchen area. And she'd already noted the bathroom lacked water glasses.

Ugh.

She turned off the light, tossing and turning before she remembered what was also in the other room: the bottles of delicious flavored mineral water sent up by the hotel's staff as an apology.

She checked the time. It was 2:00 a.m. Surely Grayson was asleep by now. He couldn't possibly mind if she took another bottle.

She picked up her dress from where she had placed it on the bench at the foot of the bed. The selections from the hotel boutique were thoughtful and extensive but didn't include pajamas. Perhaps—she blushed— the boutique employee thought as Grayson's guest Nelle wouldn't need any.

She didn't bother with her bra, pulling the dress over her head before her courage failed her. Then, on a deep inhale, she opened the door to the living space.

The fire still burned in the hearth, the gas logs turned down to an amber glow. The flames illuminated Grayson, half sitting, half lying on the sofa.

Her heart twinged in the oddest way, in an almost pleasurable pain. He looked so…young. And vulnerable, never a word she would have associated with him. Any furrows previously in his forehead were smoothed away, his jaw relaxed, his expression still. The fire burnished his hair, creating molten gold highlights that framed his face. He dwarfed the sofa's frame, causing her guilt over taking the bedroom to spike once more.

She crept farther into the room. His laptop, still open on his lap, was in danger of slipping to the floor. Sleek and light, and very expensive. No doubt he could afford to buy and sell an entire chain of computer stores, but she'd still hate to see this machine come to a bad end. She tiptoed to the edge of the sofa, then knelt on the fluffy rug. Reaching out her hands, she gently lifted the machine—

—and stared into Grayson's eyes, open and dancing with reflected fire.

Grayson wasn't sure if he was still dreaming or awake. This certainly had all the qualities of a dream, his favorite one ever since the night of the gala. Nelle kneeling before him, her hair falling about her shoulders, her eyes wide and dark, her plump lips parted. He'd reach out his hand, cup the back of her head and pull her to him…

He was halfway to reenacting his dream when he realized it was Nelle's actual hair tangling around his fingers, Nelle's real gasp echoing in his ears. He blinked and let go, bringing his right hand up to run through his hair. One thing was for sure. He was no longer asleep.

"I'm so sorry… I was only trying to… I mean…" Nelle was babbling, as disconcerted as he was. "I didn't mean to disturb you. I wasn't…" She sat back on her heels. The fire threw her figure into relief, the dress clinging to curves outlined by the flames. "I saw the laptop and I was going to…um…" She mimed closing it and putting it on the side table.

His laptop was, indeed, about to hit the floor. He reached for it at the same time she did. Their hands met. Her gaze, a dark fathomless blue in the dim light, caught and tangled with his.

If saying good-night to her earlier had been difficult, knowing how she was just on the other side of the door, trying to find sleep now would be impossible. Not with his dream made real and within his grasp, not with her soft and warm and looking at him as if they were the only two people in the world. His groin tightened as he sat up on the sofa, slipped the computer from her grip and placed it on the table, holding her gaze with his. She was so close, all he had to do was lean forward and his mouth would be on hers, his tongue free to plunder her sweetness.

"Nelle."

"Yes?" she breathed.

"Either you go back to the other room or I'm going to kiss you. Your choice."

Her eyebrows rose while her delectable lips formed a perfect O. Then she rose on her knees as if preparing to get to her feet and leave.

That was the best option. He didn't have time for a relationship, and he didn't indulge in flings, finding there was always a hidden cost even when both parties had the most casual of intentions. And even if he did practice one-night stands as a matter of course, he wasn't sure he could do that with Nelle. He meant what he said to Evan. He liked her. He didn't want to hurt her, and she was already suspicious of him as it was, thanks to whatever she thought happened between their fathers.

On the other hand, if he didn't kiss her, he wasn't

quite sure he would survive the night with his sanity intact. "Well?" he growled.

Her eyelashes fluttered and she got to her feet. She was walking away. Disappointment surged. But before it could swamp him, she returned and sat on the sofa next to him. In one hand she held the plate of chocolate-covered strawberries.

"I'm hungry," she said simply, putting it on the side table next to her. Then she picked up a strawberry and bit into it. With the berry's juice still glistening on her lips, she turned to face him and placed her lips next to his. "But not for food," she whispered against him.

He was starving. Starving for her, for the unique delight she and only she provided. His mouth met hers, the taste of strawberry and chocolate swirling around him as her tongue coaxed him deeper, harder. If kissing her in public had been thrilling, kissing her in private, with no one to see them except for a curious owl or coyote prowling past the windows, was pure erotic exhilaration.

They quickly became dissatisfied with the relatively chaste positions afforded by kissing while seated side by side. Her hands tangled in his hair as she straddled him where he sat on the sofa, her soft thighs on either side of him. He cupped her luscious ass, the slide of her velvet dress against his palms adding a new sensory thrill.

At the first taste of strawberry his cock sat straight up. With every stroke of her tongue he grew harder. Then he raised his hands to cup her breasts, her curves spilling over his palms, her nipples pushing against the velvet. He never knew his erection could be this heavy, this demanding. He took his mouth away from hers.

Her heavy-lidded eyes opened, her gaze dark and dreamy. "What is it?" she rasped, her chest rising and falling rapidly.

"We should stop now."

Some of the dreaminess left her expression. "Do you want to stop?"

No. No, he did not. He wanted to pull the velvet of her dress aside, draw her pebbled nipples into his mouth. He wanted to free his erection from its cloth prison and watch her berry-colored lips close around it. He wanted to lay her down on the sheepskin rug, open those soft thighs and draw her into his mouth, watch her scream her pleasure as the fire's glow burnished her skin. "It's late. You have a big meeting tomorrow."

"That's not a no." She rocked against him, her center pressing against his hungry cock, with only thin material separating them "Besides, are you sure I don't have something big now?" She grinned at him.

He cupped her face with his hands. "I want you. But I don't want you to think I planned this—"

She leaned forward and kissed him, taking the rest of his words away. "I know. I didn't plan this, either. But we're here. And I think I'm going to explode if we don't continue." She began to unbutton his shirt, her hands slipping below the cloth to caress his chest. Her thumbs found his nipples and she rubbed lazy circles around and over them.

If he thought his cock was already as hard as it could get, he was wrong. She wasn't the only one about to explode, and they were still mostly clothed. "If you insist," he managed to grind out.

She kissed a path from his jaw to his ear. "If you're really concerned about my rest, orgasms help me sleep." Then she slid off him, standing in the firelight. He watched, mesmerized, as she pulled her dress over her head. She wore nothing underneath.

Her breasts were even more beautiful than he imagined. Perfect round globes tipped with dark rose nipples that begged to be suckled and worshipped. Dark curls clustered in the V between her legs, below an hourglass waist and set off by beautifully curved wide hips. She smiled at him. "It's your turn."

She didn't have to ask twice. But he had more clothes than her. He busied himself shedding garments, looking up as he pulled off his shoes. She wasn't there. He frowned and stood up to look for her. "Nelle? Everything okay? Did you change your mind?"

"Of course not." She emerged from the bathroom off the living area. "I was looking though the amenity basket."

"Oh? Sudden craving for shower gel? Or a sewing kit?"

She bit her lower lip. "Well, I was thinking. I don't have condoms with me. I was hoping the hotel bathroom had some, but no. Or…you?"

He hadn't carried condoms in his wallet since he graduated college. "No."

"Oh." Then her gaze landed on him, almost fully nude. His male ego was gratified by how her eyes widened, her pupils dilating as she stared her fill. "You, um, still have one sock on," she choked out.

"Easily rectified." He moved to the sofa to sit down and remove it. "Unless the lack of condom made you change your mind."

She shook her head rapidly and moved to kneel in front of him, taking his foot into her hand. "Allow me."

She slowly rolled his sock down his ankle, her slender fingers caressing his skin as it was revealed. He bit back a groan. Who knew the lower leg was a major erogenous zone? His erection pulsed as she ever so gently tugged the article free.

She sat back on her heels and regarded him from under her eyelashes. "While I have you here... I've been thinking about this since the night of the gala. And considering we don't have condoms..."

She leaned forward. And then her mouth was on his erection, her wet, unbelievably hot mouth. She drew him in, her tongue swirling and licking, her fingers stroking, somehow knowing exactly how much pressure was needed and where to apply it to make him see stars behind his eyelids. He thought his fantasies were scorching, but the real thing was beyond anything his imagination was capable of conjuring. The pressure built before he knew it, demanding release and so he tugged her up, sweeping her the short distance to the sheepskin rug before them. He was not willing to end this night with her so soon. He had no idea if there would be another. This one shouldn't even be happening. But since it was, he wanted to make every minute last.

It was his turn to indulge his fantasy and so he gently laid her before the fire, kissing and nipping his way from her breasts to her inner thighs, stroking the soft skin and inhaling the sea salt scent he discovered there. Then he licked into her, finding her clit and ensuring it received the attention from his mouth that it deserved. She trembled, her breathing turning harsh and heavy, her hips starting to buck, and he let her guide him to what pleased her most until she shuddered and cried out. He traveled back up her torso, kissing the same path he had taken on the way down. Then he lay beside her, propped up on one elbow, tracing patterns on the gentle hill of her stomach as she came back to herself.

As he watched, something unfurled in Grayson. Something that had been present before, but easy to ignore. Now it straightened out, grew shoots, the roots digging in deeper.

He liked her. He really liked her.

This couldn't come at a worse time.

Her eyelashes fluttered. "Okay. That was…okay."

"Okay?" He grinned at her. "First you called my kiss adequate, now this was okay?"

She shook her head. "I mean, okay, let me get my breath back. Pretty sure it's in Nevada."

He kissed her forehead. "One orgasm, delivered. Do you think you can sleep now?"

She gave him a sleepy smile. "Maybe. But I hate to go to sleep with a guilty conscience."

He laughed. "What do you have to feel guilty about?"

"Unfinished business." She reached down between them, her fingers closing around his cock and finding his most sensitive places to stroke. He groaned and lay back. This time, he allowed her to complete what she had started earlier, coming so violently he was pretty sure he passed out for a minute or two. Then he guided her back to the bed, ensured she was tucked in tight, and fell asleep with his arm curving around her waist.

Until the phone rang, less than two hours later.

Seven

Nelle ignored the ringing phone, choosing to go back to her very compelling dream. She was in bed with Grayson Monk. Desire lit his golden-brown gaze. His mouth covered hers before moving to her neck, her breasts, and down her stomach—

The phone rang again. Nelle groaned and rolled over, punching her fist into the oddly hard pillow to find a more comfortable spot.

A loud male grunt caused her eyes to fly open.

Her head wasn't on a pillow, but a firm, warm and very male chest. She raised her head to find the object of her dream gazing down at her, sleepy amusement in his gaze.

"Good morning to you, too. And I think that's your phone."

"Sorry." Her brain went into overdrive, vibrating between two thoughts. She was in bed with Grayson. She had a meeting.

She. Was. In. Bed. With. Grayson.

And she was naked.

She pulled the sheets around her, scrambling to put some distance between them, only for Grayson to tug her head back down to his for a long, senses-drugging kiss. She blinked at him when he broke contact. What was she supposed to be doing again? His kiss drove all thoughts away.

He reached across her, found her ringing phone on the bedside table, and handed it to her. She took it from him with a discomfited smile. "Thanks." Then she looked at the screen and threw back the covers, heedless of her state of undress. "It's my alarm. For my meeting with Reid Begaye."

Grayson's gaze followed her as she gathered up the bags from the hotel boutique and ran-walked to the bathroom. She fought the urge to hide every imperfect bump and crease from his view, as she did when she had lived with Harry. Last night she'd done her best to embrace her new philosophy, telling herself to act confident, bold, unashamed.

Only she didn't have to act. He made her feel beautiful—no, that wasn't it, exactly. He made her feel like she was enough. Enough to be desired. Enough to be worshipped.

Enough for him.

Nelle liked being enough. It was a good change, feeling she didn't have to apologize for not being prettier or smarter or more sophisticated. And she had never been so aware of a man's appreciative gaze before. Harry's gaze hadn't lingered and it had certainly never caressed.

She could bathe in the light shining in Grayson's eyes all day.

She exited the bathroom, clad in gray fine wool trousers and a navy blue cashmere sweater so fine it floated over her skin as if spun from mist by angels. Grayson was in the living room, intent on his laptop. He was also shaved and showered thanks to the second bathroom, his dark blond hair showing the tracks of the comb he'd used to tame it for the time being. It was hard to believe the man who looked every inch a Silicon Valley executive in his crisp white shirt, sport coat and tailored trousers was the man whose skin she had explored with her fingers, lips, tongue.

"Hey," she said, a tentativeness she didn't feel when they were naked descending on her now that they were both clothed.

He looked up, his gaze distant at first but sharpening to appreciation as he took in her appearance. "My compliments to whoever picked out that sweater."

She did a slow pirouette. "This is okay for meeting Reid?"

"Okay is a highly inadequate description."

She tucked a lock of hair behind her ear. "I'm going to go to my breakfast now. I…" This was where she usually stammered and hesitated, wondering if he would ask to see her again, agonizing if he would call or text her. She hated one-night stands. She never got the hang of divorcing her expectations from the act of having sex. She wished she could learn how to enjoy a good time and walk away, chalking up the experience as a one-and-done moment in time.

But she had no other choice. She was not getting involved with a Monk. Sure, they had amazing chemistry, and now they knew it resulted in amazing sex. That should be enough. It would have to be enough.

She straightened her shoulders and held out her right hand. "I want to formally say goodbye, since the last time we…kissed… I rudely ran away. I can't thank you enough for inviting me to the wine tasting. And I'll send a check to your office for my new outfit." After getting an advance on her paycheck, that was.

Grayson looked at her outstretched palm, and then stood up without taking it. "That sounds final."

"Well, I mean…that is…" Damn it. She was babbling. Again. She took a deep breath, trying to force herself to meet his gaze and failing miserably. "We're both adults. Adults have sex. It doesn't mean anything."

He took her hand then, but instead of shaking it he used it to pull her in close. She resisted the urge to close her eyes and lean into him. Lean into him and wrap her arms around his neck and not let go for a very long time. "Then that's where we're different. It does mean something to me," he said.

Her gaze flew to meet his. "Wait. It does?"

He caressed her jawline with his thumb, then cupped the back of her head and brought her mouth to his for a long, deep kiss. He lifted his head just enough to speak against her lips. "It does."

Then he let go of her and returned to the low sofa, picking up his laptop again. "But if you don't feel the same way, I'll respect that. Either way, I'll be in the lobby after your meeting to make sure you get home."

She wasn't sure she could form coherent sentences after that kiss, much less make a cogent pitch for the nonprofit. But the promise in his words that this wasn't a one-night stand and he wanted to see her again—later today, even!—carried her on a cloud of hope she didn't even dare express to herself.

Reid was charming. There was no other word to describe him. At another time, in another place, he would have swept Nelle off her feet. He was smart and witty and listened intently to what she had to say. His questions were intelligent and pointed, and he made astute observations. Although it lasted well over two hours, at any other point in time breakfast would have flown by for Nelle.

But it didn't fly by, because every minute was a minute she anticipated seeing Grayson again. The anticipation made the hands on her watch seem to move so slowly that it felt as if a turtle could have completed a marathon between every tick.

Then Reid promised to pledge at least two million dollars from his foundation toward the completion of Create4All's new facility. That got her attention. Their conversation shifted to outlining the next steps.

Well, it got most of her attention.

"We'll have to see your books." Reid folded his napkin and put it down on the table next to his plate. "We need to ensure Create4All meets with the foundation's standards and guidelines for financial transparency and program spending. I'll warn you now, they're very stringent."

"Of course," Nelle agreed, folding her own napkin and placing it on the table. She'd barely touched her cheese omelet. "I'm sure the board of directors will be thrilled to give you all the information you require."

Reid nodded. "I'll have my grant director get in touch. Let me send a few emails while I'm thinking of it." He took out his phone, tapped on the screen for a few minutes, then rose from the table to help Nelle out of her chair. "I hate to leave so abruptly after such a great discussion, but."

"I understand." She smiled. "Break a leg at the keynote."

"More like break heads. The heads of the people I'm speaking to, that is. They're not going to like what I have to say to them." He smiled and held out his hand. "I'm not just saying this. I enjoyed our breakfast."

His large hand enveloped hers, his grip firm and warm. But no sparks traveled from where their hands met. The air remained free of electrical charge. "I did, too."

He nodded at the business card clutched in her hand. "You know where to find me Now tell Grayson he can call off the rescue party."

"Rescue party?"

Reid nodded at the nearby entrance to the restaurant. "He's been pacing in the lobby, glaring at me though those glass doors."

"He's what?" She swiveled in her chair to look behind her. Grayson was indeed in the lobby, but he was seated in a chair, speaking to what looked like a fellow conference attendee. But as soon as she spotted him, he looked up, catching her gaze with an easy smile.

Her stomach clenched, then fluttered in response.

"Okay, so he just sat down," Reid said. "Anyway, like I said, you know where to find me. See you around." He gave her a tip of his Stetson before he exited.

Nelle stayed seated, gathering her thoughts before she joined Grayson in the lobby. The image of his smile lingered before her. This was bad. She was more excited about the prospect of being in his company than she had ever been waking up on her birthday.

Be cool. Sure, last night had been amazing. But the lack of a condom had stopped them from exploring more of each other. Maybe he said those things to her so he could have the full experience before discarding her. Because he would. That's what Monks did to people like her.

Or at least, that's what his father did. Maybe—she glanced back at Grayson, who was engrossed in his conversation—maybe that didn't have to be their fate. After all, he said their night together meant something to him.

If she were being honest, it meant more to her than she could describe as well.

When she finally entered the lobby, Grayson broke off his discussion and stood up to greet her.

"Meeting go well?"

There was his grin. It warmed her insides, causing them to melt to the consistency of marshmallow fluff. All thoughts to channel her inner Elsa and cool their interaction in an avalanche of ice melted away. "It did. Better than any of my expectations. Thank you again."

"I had nothing to do with it. If Reid is making a donation, that's all your doing." He moved closer. Her nose caught notes of grapefruit and blood orange from toiletries provided by the hotel, plus a scent she recognized from the night before as uniquely his. Indescribable in words, but she would know it was him in the pitch dark.

Which made her think of other things she'd like to do to him in the dark. And in the daylight. At twilight. During the late afternoon. Or midmorning, like now. *Damn it.* Last night should have lessened the urge. Dissipated the heat that seemed to materialize every time they were close enough to touch. Instead, the flames leaped even higher. "Still, you deserve my thanks. For bringing me. And for, well, last night. I mean, providing a place to stay. Among other things."

His mouth turned up in a lopsided smile. "I should be thanking you. After all, you saved my computer from a possibly fatal fall. Among other things."

She wanted to run her fingers along his stubbled

jawline, explore with her own mouth where his smile dented his left cheek. She settled for, "My pleasure. Especially the...other things."

His gaze darkened, the golden shards in his irises standing out in bright relief. "I would very much like a physical demonstration of those other things, just to make sure we're on the same page. Unfortunately, I need to immediately return to San Francisco. The valet is pulling my car around now."

"Oh." She didn't know why her skin ran cold, as if an immense gray cloud dumped stinging rain on her head.

"I can give drive you home," he continued. "But I have to stop by my place in the city first. There's a video conference call I need to take from my home office. If you want to go straight home or to Create4All, I can have the driver take you instead."

The cloud lifted. She tilted her head to one side as she pretended to ponder the choice. "You know, I'd love to see more of San Francisco. The gala was my first time back in the city in years."

"If you don't mind waiting for my call to finish, I'm happy to play tour guide after." He offered his left elbow to her and escorted her to the lushly landscaped front entrance of the hotel, where his Tesla Model S awaited. The bellman placed a bag bearing the hotel boutique's label in the trunk as she sank down on the smooth leather of the passenger seat, marveling at the large touch screen that served as the car's dashboard. In some ways, the car was a metaphor for Grayson: sleek, unexpected, startling.

If she had a car capable of driving itself like a Tesla, she would get into trouble. She would let her guard down and put too much trust in it. She wouldn't be safe.

The same was true of Grayson. If she kept giving in to the temptation of his company, she was going to be in serious trouble. Although, if she were being honest, she'd flown past the signs warning of danger as soon as she opened the door to the bedroom last night.

They managed to drive to San Francisco without incident despite the distraction of being seated next to each other, close enough to run her hand along his thigh, near enough for him to lean over and capture her mouth at every red light. When they reached his place, a penthouse condominium on top of Nob Hill, she thrummed with desire. It was almost a relief when he left her in the open living area, promising to return as soon as he finished the call in his office. It allowed her to think straight again.

His home occupied the entire top floor of his building and was furnished in a masculine, minimalist style. Dark leather furniture and ebony wood shelves stood out against creamy white walls, decorated at intervals with abstract paintings featuring bold splashes of color.

She wandered to the floor-to-ceiling windows that lined one wall, offering panoramic vistas of the city below and the bay beyond. She had a bird's-eye view, and as if to illustrate the point, a seagull flew past as she watched tiny sailboats bob in the distant dark blue water.

Next to her stood an accent table with a display of several photos. She picked up one at random. A black-and-white Grayson smiled back at her. He stood next to his sister, who shared his square jaw and dark eyes.

Standing on the other side of Grayson in the photo—her heart skipped a beat—was his father. She'd recognize Barrett anywhere. From him, Grayson inherited his easy smile and dark blond surfer hair.

She ran a finger across Barrett's face, wondering how the demon of her bedtime stories could look so… normal. So relaxed, so happy to be with his children. Not a fang or evil eye in sight. But she knew the damage he'd done to her family. At least, she thought she did. The last week had turned her preconceptions upside down, inside out and sideways.

Perhaps Grayson was right. They were all the protagonists of their own individual stories. In telling a story that made himself the hero, did her father cast Barrett as the villain undeservedly?

"That was taken at Dad's last victory party," Grayson said from behind her.

"I wondered at the balloons. You, and your sister both look too old for it to be a birthday celebration."

"And just as I locked in the balloon shipment for my next birthday."

She laughed and put the photo down. "Is your meeting over? That was fast."

He made a noncommittal noise. "It's over for me. I have more pressing items to take care of."

"Take as much time as you need. I'm enjoying the view." She indicated the panoramic city scene before her.

"So am I."

She glanced up to realize his gaze was not focused on the hustle and bustle of the streets below them, but on her. A warm flush traveled from her cheeks to her chest.

"And the first urgent item on my agenda," he continued, "is the sightseeing I promised you." He came to join her at the window, his left arm brushing her right, causing the tiny hairs on her skin to rise up.

"I feel like I'm getting an aerial tour from here. Look, there's the Bay Bridge. And Treasure Island." She raised her right hand to point.

"That's Yerba Buena Island. Treasure Island is next to it." He took her hand in his, moving it a fraction of an inch. "Here," he said, low into her ear.

She shivered as his breath whispered against her cheek. "And the smaller island over there?"

"Alcatraz."

She knew that. But she liked having an excuse to keep her hand in his. "What about the building shaped like a cylinder?" She turned her head to look at him.

Their mouths were millimeters apart.

"Coit Tower," he said.

"And that one?" She had no idea what she pointed at. She was focused on his lips, firm and beautifully shaped. Her mouth fit against his as if they were two pieces of the same puzzle. She suddenly very much wanted to kiss him again.

"I'm guessing… Transamerica Pyramid."

"You don't know?" Her gaze rose to meet his. Then her breath seized at the sheer want in his gaze. Want. For her.

"You're all I see right now." He lifted the back of his hand to her cheek, his thumb caressing the curve of her jaw.

Her heart skipped a beat then sped up, a timpani played at lightning speed.

"All I want right now is you," she managed to get out, and then she was kissing him, or he was kissing her. She didn't care, she only wanted the sweep of his tongue in hers, to suckle on his tongue in return.

The night before had been a waking dream. Midnight dark, the world silent and fast asleep, exploring each other on a luxurious rug in front of the fire: it was easy to tell herself sex with him was a once-in-a-lifetime indulgence of her imagination. The chance to fulfill her teenage wishful thinking, hero worshipping the hometown national swim star from afar.

But it had been pure fantasy, in a hotel bungalow that cost more per night than her share of monthly rent. Even as she shuddered underneath his insistent mouth, she refused to believe it had been real.

But now… He lifted her sweater and she helped him remove it, breaking their kiss just long enough to pull it over her head. Then they were kissing again, his hands cupping her breasts, stroking her through her bra, her nipples hard and aching and begging for more. Then her bra was off and he gave her nipples what she desired, pulling them into his mouth, rolling them with his tongue.

She took the first chance she had to unbutton his shirt and tug it free from the trousers. He was now sporting a very impressive bulge. She caressed him through the fabric of his pants, loving the way he jerked against her, his arms pulling her tight against him, trapping her between him and the window. She gasped as her bare back met the glass, her superheated skin and the cold surface combining to shock her into even more awareness.

He glanced up from where he was unbuttoning her trousers. She stared back at him, unable to talk, only able feel the smooth coolness behind her, his warm fingers at her belly, her breasts bare and exposed to the air. He tugged her trousers down and then she was nude, save for the tiny wisp of silk covering her sex.

Despite the bright sunlight streaming in from the windows, his eyes dilated deepest black as they took in her newly acquired lingerie. "Is that from the hotel?"

She nodded, still unable to draw in enough oxygen to speak.

"Remind me to send whoever chose your clothes a thank-you card."

Then he was on his knees, his mouth kissing her though the soaked silk. His right hand came up to hold her still, pressed against the glass, as his right hand brushed the flimsy panty aside. Then his tongue and fingers took turns, licking, pressing, circling. It didn't take long. She had been on fire for him since the moment she punched him that morning. She gave herself over to the spiraling demand, crying his name as she came.

She would have fallen if it weren't for his arms. He held her up, stroking her back as she collapsed against him.

But she wouldn't let him see just how thoroughly he'd burned through all her defenses. How she was already halfway to being in love with him. She lifted her head and gave him a crooked smile. "That was decent."

"Decent, adequate, okay—I might develop a complex." He nipped at her earlobe.

"I like what's developing here." The bulge in his trousers was larger than before. She squeezed it gently, receiving a groan in return. "Please tell me you have condoms."

"Left pocket," he grunted. "Put them there after my phone call."

She slipped her hand into his pocket, brushing against his erection through the pocket lining as she did. He jerked against her.

"Let's get you undressed. And then dressed again." She carefully unzipped his fly, then pushed down his trousers and briefs. His erection sprung into her hand and she reveled in rolling on the condom, loving the velvet smoothness, the heavy firmness. "Bedroom?" she whispered against his lips when she was done.

He smiled, and the wickedness lurking there made her gasp with anxious anticipation. He kissed her, hard, deep, then turned her in his arms so she faced the window and he was at her back. "Since you seemed to like this last time," he rumbled in her ear. "Don't worry, the building was retrofitted for earthquakes. Not even an eight point zero will make this window fall out."

"I'm pretty sure that last one was a ten," she gasped, and then she stopped forming coherent thoughts as he pressed her forward until her breasts grazed the glass, her already hard nipples puckering to points of painful pleasure. He nudged her knees apart and her palms flew up to rest flat against the window for support. Then he was at her entrance. Thick. Large. Demanding.

She cried out as he filled her. He rested his head against hers for a beat, letting her adjust to his size. Then he began to move, long strokes, hard strokes, building in heat and intensity. His arm came around to hold her, pulling her against him, helping her set the rhythm she required. His breathing was harsh in her ear, his scent surrounding her. Her knees started to tremble and he increased his tempo, pushing faster and faster. Her orgasm began to build again, a softly rolling one this time. Then he brought one of her icy hands down from the window to the front of her sex, pressed her cold fingers against her clit.

The orgasm hit her like a freight train without brakes. Then he shuddered against her, his movements gradually slowing until they collapsed together on a deep pile rug.

"I bet we shocked some pigeons," she said when speech returned to her.

"Someday we have to try that in a bed."

She glanced over at him. "My schedule is free for the rest of the day."

He shrugged. "I have an appointment to take someone sightseeing."

She lazily pointed at the windows. "You already showed me. San Francisco is that way. Your job is done."

"Well, there's one more place I might want to show you. And by coincidence, it happens to have a bed."

She got to her feet, still unsure whether her legs could support her weight. "Where do I buy my ticket for this tour?"

Eight

Grayson watched as Nelle slept, burrowing deeper into the covers as protection against the chilly morning air. He gathered her against him, luxuriating in the feel of her skin against his, smooth to his rough, and inhaling her spicy-sweet scent. Maybe he could call in sick. Maybe he could persuade her to call in sick and they could play hooky for the day, have a long, fortifying breakfast to make up for the meals they'd missed in favor of staying in bed. But even as he played around with the thought, he dismissed it. Nelle took her job at Create4All seriously. And he had too much work to do as it was. Starting with an early-morning meeting with—

"Hello? Grayson? You here?"

Damn it. Finley. He knew it had been a mistake to give her the access codes to his home.

"Grayson? You can't possibly still be sleeping."

Nelle stirred beside him, then bolted awake. "Did I hear someone?" she whispered to him.

"It's my sister. Stay here. I'll get rid of her." He kissed her on the forehead. Then he threw on a pair of old sweatpants and headed to the kitchen, where Finley was making herself a cappuccino. Badly.

"You're going to break that," he warned, and took over from her.

"I don't know why you have a car with no visible controls and a coffee machine that looks like something NASA uses to land vehicles on Mars," Finley complained.

Grayson prepared a cup of steaming caffeine for her, then made one for himself. "We aren't supposed to meet until this afternoon. Why are you here?"

"Now that's an interesting question," she said. "Almost as interesting as what you did this weekend."

"I was here for most of it." Not a lie.

"As has been noted." She handed him her phone. "By the way, do be careful when you leave. There are some rather persistent paparazzi who want a follow-up photo, so your building's exits are staked out. The doormen can only do so much."

"What are you talking about?" Then he looked at her phone screen—and saw red. "What the hell is this?"

Finley tapped her chin with her right index finger. "I have to confess, when we discussed campaign girlfriends, I didn't think you would jump at the idea so eagerly."

Grayson stared at the phone. Finley's web browser was open to the gossip page for *Silicon Valley Weekly*. And there, filling the screen, was a photo of him and Nelle at the wine tasting, their gazes locked on each other, the angle of the photo making it look as if they were just about to kiss. Next to it, much smaller, was the previously published photo of the two of them, in their masquerade finery, in Embarcadero Plaza. "CINDERELLA UNMASKED" screamed the headline in bold, stark lettering.

"It's a nice photo, isn't it?" Finley said, peering over his shoulder at the phone. "They got your good side." She took the phone from his nerveless grip and opened a note-taking app. "Must remember to remind other photographers to do the same."

"Did you do this?" He was surprised how calm he sounded. Still, Finley took a step back.

"Do what?"

"This. Place this story."

She rolled her eyes. "No, Grayson, I did not. If you don't want your photo on gossip websites, then don't continue to kiss people in public places. You're a person of interest. It's just going to intensify on Wednesday when Dad steps down."

"I may be a person of interest, but she isn't. This is your only warning. Leave her out of—wait. Did you say Wednesday?"

"That's when Dad is announcing his resignation."

What the... "That's the day after tomorrow. It was supposed to be next month."

"Change of plans." Finley busied herself adding sugar to her cappuccino. "And before you ask, the change is final."

No. He needed more time, damn it. Time to wrap up his business. Time to discover if the connection he felt with Nelle was real.

It wasn't on his agenda to date someone. And he didn't have flings. It was why he was so successful as an investor: he only committed once he was sure, and then he worked hard at making the partnership a success.

It had been a mistake to give in to the temptation of a sleep-warmed Nelle, kneeling before him with fire reflected in her gaze. To indulge the rush of need that engulfed him as she stood next to him, her fingers trembling in his. The wisest course forward would be to cut off the relationship now, before the hooks became more deeply embedded in his heart.

Right now, only one commitment mattered. And that was the one he made to his family. But he could try to claw back as much time for himself as he could. "We have a deal, Fin."

"Tell Dad's heart and the episodes of tachycardia he keeps having that you have a deal. He could have hit his head when he fainted over the weekend—" She clapped her right hand over her mouth. "I'm sorry, he didn't want me to tell you. He doesn't want you distracted."

"Dad fainted?" The room appeared to revolve.

Grayson grabbed the back of a nearby chair for balance. "He sounded fine last time we spoke. His doctors said he was well on the way to recovering."

"He is. He will." Finley sighed. "But I believe the resignation hanging over his head is causing the tachycardia. That's why we're moving it up."

Grayson shook his head, still trying to process the new information. "You should have told me. *He* should have told me."

"And if we told you, you would've dropped everything to visit him, and then we'd have even less time to prep for the campaign launch. He thought it was for the best."

"You agreed with him?"

She bit her lower lip. "It doesn't matter what I think," she finally said. "This is about you and him and the Monk legacy. I'm just the facilitator. My job is to make the way smooth for him and now for you."

"You're not a facilitator, you're my sister. His daughter."

"If you want to get my titles correct, I'm your half-sister. His stepdaughter." Something cold and dark flashed in Finley's gaze. "And I'm also your campaign manager and his chief of staff until he resigns. Let's keep our eyes on the prize, which is your election."

"The election isn't more important than family—"

Finley scoffed. "This *is* family. If you lose you might not be disowned, but I definitely will be."

"C'mon, Fin. You know that's not true."

She opened her mouth, then shut it with a snap. Then she smiled, the kind of smile he recognized from long experience meant trouble for the person on the receiving end. "So, let's talk Cinderella. Is she the one until the election or do we still need to find you a campaign girlfriend?"

"A campaign *what*?"

Ice water replaced the blood in Grayson's veins. He turned, dreading what he knew he would see.

Nelle stood in doorway, dressed in his robe. At any other time, the sight of her wearing an article of his clothing—the sleeves falling down to cover her hands, the tie wound several times around her waist to keep the voluminous fabric somewhat contained— would have made him grin. Then he would sweep her up in his arms and carry her back to bed.

Now, he ran through various responses, discarding them as quickly as they popped into his head. No, she wasn't hearing things. No, she shouldn't leave and he'd explain later. No, Finley wasn't making a bad joke.

His sister broke the silence that hung in the air after Nelle's question. She held out her right hand for a handshake. "Hi, we saw each other in Grayson's office but I don't think we've been formally introduced. I'm Finley Smythe."

"Nelle Lassen." Nelle held herself as if she were clothed in couture rather than his bathrobe. "Or perhaps I should say Cinder-Nelle-a?"

Finley broke into a delighted smile. "That's good." She turned to Grayson. "Keep this one. I can work with funny."

The arch smile on his sister's face shook him out

of his impersonation of a statue. "You're not going to do anything of the sort," he warned, picking up Finley's mostly untouched cappuccino and placing it in the sink. "Thanks for literally dropping in but call next time." He turned to Nelle, his heart thudding in his ears. "Let's get dressed, go out for breakfast, and I'll explain."

She ignored him and his stomach sank further. She perched on one of the barstools at the island that separated the kitchen from the informal eating area, rolling up the sleeves of the bathrobe and crossing her long legs as if sitting down for the final round of deal negotiations in the boardroom. "Work with that how?" she asked Finley.

"You know Grayson's going to run for Congress, right? I'm assuming he told you."

Nelle nodded. "Yes, for your father's seat."

Finley clasped her hands together and beamed. "So I'm going to be your fairy godmother. For the duration of the campaign."

"All right. Enough is enough." Grayson picked up Finley's tote bag and thrust it at her. "Goodbye."

"Grayson, it's okay." Nelle caught his gaze. To his stunned amazement, she wasn't upset or angry or even shocked. Instead, humor lurked in her blue gaze. "I've always wanted a fairy godmother," she said to Finley. "What does that entail, precisely?"

"First, I need to know if you are committed. To the campaign, that is. What you and my brother decide to do afterward is your affair. Pun fully intended."

"Gee, thanks for that," Grayson deadpanned.

"Nelle, would you like an espresso or a cappuccino? Alcohol optional." Irish coffee was supposedly invented in San Francisco. Probably because the bartender had a sister like Finley.

"Would caffeine help make sense of this conversation?" Nelle asked him.

He shook his head. "No. I'm hoping the addition of whiskey will."

"So, are you?" Finley persisted. "Committed to helping us with the campaign?"

"Don't say anything," Grayson suggested to Nelle. "If we ignore her, maybe she'll go away."

Nelle leaned her elbows on the island's marble counter. The bathrobe gaped open, teasing his gaze until she pulled it closed. "I can't commit to something if I don't know what it is."

"Date my brother. Until the general election is over."

"I might not make it that far," Grayson interjected. At least Nelle seemed to be taking the conversation in stride. He might as well try to do the same thing. And then they could hopefully laugh about it in the future. *If* they had a future. The fact that Nelle still sat in his kitchen was the only thing keeping Finley employed as his campaign manager.

"When you make it," Finley corrected him, then addressed Nelle. "I'm not asking you to do anything different from what you're apparently doing now, judging by your current ensemble." She waved a hand at the bathrobe Nelle wore. "Just don't break up with him until the winner is announced."

"What if I said your brother very kindly offered to let me crash here and this isn't what it seems?" Nelle accepted the mug Grayson handed her with a grateful smile.

"See?" He raised an eyebrow at Finley. "Logical explanation for Nelle's presence, so there is no need to involve her in your machinations. We can strategize about the campaign later. Right now, Nelle and I both need to shower, get dressed and go to work."

"You know fully well explanation isn't synonymous with truth." His sister narrowed her gaze at him. "And I'm not leaving until I get my answer. Look, your sentiment score has steadily climbed since the story broke late last night. People really like the idea of you and Cinderella." She held out her phone, the screen exhibiting a line graph trending upward.

"Sentiment score—do I want to know what that is?"

"Grayson, you need to start reading the materials I'm sending you—"

Nelle took a long sip from her mug, watching the siblings argue, thankful to be forgotten for the minute. It was one of the most delicious cappuccinos she'd ever had. Trust Grayson to even make hot beverages more amazing than she could have imagined.

She hadn't planned on intruding on his conversation with Finley. Nelle had been warm and cozy in his bed, propped up by enormous goose down pillows while texting Yoselin not to expect her in the office until the afternoon. But then an email had come in from Reid Begaye. She was so excited by its contents she only had one thought: to share it with Grayson. After all, he was the one who made the introduction. So she'd followed the sound of the voices, intending to wait until he had finished with his visitor.

Then she heard the word "girlfriend." Suddenly, interrupting him was of prime importance.

She wasn't really considering Finley's proposal to date Grayson for the duration of the campaign, was she? Yes, they had explosive chemistry. Even now, despite his sister's presence, it took everything she had not to run her hands over the well-defined pectoral muscles on display, let her fingers follow the dusting of dark blond hair from his six-pack abs to where it trailed into his low-slung sweatpants.

But no chemical reaction lasted forever, right? She ignored the tiny voice in the back of her head exclaiming this was more than mere lust.

Her old self would have rejected the suggestion that she date someone for an ulterior motive—and not just someone. A member of the Monk family. Janelle's indignant nose would be in the air as she stormed out in huff. And rightfully so.

What Barrett had done to her father was unconscionable. She could recite the story by heart. When the client funds were discovered missing, Barrett had produced a second set up of financial books that showed her father made the withdrawals. Her father had searched but couldn't find the real records. He'd narrowly escaped jail, but his legal career was over. And if he had turned to gambling to make extra money, so what? What other choices did he have?

Her parents had fought constantly over finances and her father's drinking at the gaming tables until her mother finally left when Nelle was in ninth grade. If it weren't for her late grandmother, who ensured she graduated high school and received a scholarship to college... Nelle didn't want to think about how her life would be different.

She came by her hatred of Barrett honestly.

But so much had happened over the last week. The gala, the trip to Napa, the aching tenderness of the night before. The look in Grayson's eyes when he said their time together meant something to him. The inalienable truths of her world were being torn down and worn away.

A sudden lull in the argument appeared and she seized the opening. "I have a question."

Finley and Grayson swung their heads to look at her, both sets of eyebrows raised.

"What does it matter if Grayson is dating someone or not? Do the voters of El Santo really care that much about his love life?"

Finley laughed. "You wouldn't ask if you knew El Santo."

"Nelle grew up there," Grayson informed her.

Finley's eyes widened so much she reminded Nelle of an animated film character. "Oh, this can't get any better. Really?"

"Go Saints," Nelle said, referring to the local high school team's football team.

"Then you should know the answer to your question," Finley responded.

Yeah. Nelle did. It was one of the reasons why she'd left as soon as she could and never returned. A town that placed a premium on appearances was not kind to a child whose mother ran off with a married man and whose father was more often found in the dive bars outside the city limits than he was at his paralegal desk. It was why she threw cold water at the thought of Grayson running for his father's seat when speaking to Yoselin at the gala. Barrett Monk had done nothing to help El Santo face the realities of the changing world, choosing instead to bolster the residents' illusions and stoke their resentments. El Santo deserved a representative who sought to provide what the people needed, not promise them what they thought they wanted and could never receive.

But Grayson, as he reminded her several times, was not his father.

She addressed Finley. "Speaking of El Santo, you should know I'm Doug Lassen's daughter."

Finley's expression remined blank. "Is there a reason that should mean something to me?"

"Nelle's father and Barrett have a long-ago history," Grayson replied.

"Barrett was my father's legal partner and my father was disbarred when their practice broke up," Nelle said evenly, refusing to look at Grayson. She knew he still didn't believe Barrett had set her father up. No need to go into the details with Finley.

Finley thought for a second. "I like it," she said.

"If Cinderella starts to feel played out in the media, we can use Romeo and Juliet."

"Stop—" Grayson warned.

Finley held up a hand. "Fine, no Shakespearean tragedies." She turned to Nelle. "This is the first I've heard of your father. And if I don't know, then Barrett doesn't care. But if you think this will be a problem, we'll find someone else."

"No. There won't be anyone else." Grayson put his hand on Nelle's shoulder, angling himself as if to protect her from Finley. The warmth of his touch penetrated through the plush fabric. "I don't care about sentiment scores. You need to drop this."

Finley threw up her hands. "You need to trust me. I know what I'm doing." She appealed to Nelle. "Save him from himself. Say yes."

Nelle's heart pounded. A year ago, she would have said no way to Finley's scheme. But wasn't the point of becoming New Nelle to take risks, to change her luck? Besides, she owed Grayson. A lot. He introduced her to Reid Begaye, and in the process probably saved her job.

And maybe, if she helped Grayson, she could turn around the story of the Monks and the Lassens.

Maybe it didn't have to end so badly this time.

She swiveled in her stool to face him. "Do you want this? Me, I mean. Until the election. Not that it would mean anything. Because it wouldn't. I don't want you to think that I would think—"

"Nelle." Grayson's dark gaze caught hers. For a second, they were the only two people in the room.

In the world, for that matter. "I like you. I like being with you."

Did the sun suddenly come out from behind a cloud? The entire room seemed brighter, sharper.

"Is that a yes?"

"I don't want to drag you into Finley's ridiculous scheme." But before the light could dim and winked out, he continued. "I do want to continue seeing you."

She wasn't sure if she stood up or if he pulled her off her barstool, but then she was in his arms and his mouth was on hers. Their now familiar electricity arced between them, crackling with heat.

"Fairy godmothering starts tomorrow. Be ready," Nelle heard Finley say, followed by the sound of a door closing. But then Grayson's hands were cupping her rear end, lifting her, carrying her back down the hallway to his bedroom.

It's only a favor, Nelle told herself while she was still capable of coherent thought. An opportunity to repay him while perhaps changing the trajectory of their families' entwined histories. Nothing more. But even as the words faded from her brain, replaced by a sharp jolt of pleasure as Grayson's mouth pulled on the diamond hard peak of her breast, she knew they were a lie.

Nine

Nelle ran one hand through her newly cut hair and tightened her grip on the straps of her overnight bag in the other. One deep inhale later, she knocked on the door of Grayson's temporary residence in El Santo, a sprawling ranch house on the west side of the small city.

He opened it. At the sight of his smiling face, she exhaled, dropped the bag and threw herself into his arms for a very thorough kiss. The knot between her shoulders that caused them to bunch up around her ears for the entire three-hour drive southeast from Fremont vanished, as if by magic. Crossing the city limits into El Santo was never easy for her, but as always, his presence caused her to melt into a gooey mess.

The six weeks since that fateful morning in Grayson's kitchen had been a whirlwind of nonstop activity. Barrett had announced he would not seek reelection. The governor had called a special election to be held in November. Competitors flocked to file the paperwork to run. So far, no one caused Finley particular concern, although she was keeping a wary eye on a retired rancher who owned vast tracts of land in the district. Grayson began to spend the bulk of his time in El Santo, reacquainting himself with his birthplace.

Simultaneously, Nelle's job had gone into overdrive as the contacts she made at the gala and the winery began to bear fruit. Nearly every breakfast, lunch and dinner—and the hours between—were booked with meetings and follow-up appointments and new social events. She finally had enough money saved to afford renting her own studio apartment so she could give Yoselin and Jason their privacy, but she was too busy to house-hunt. Not that Yoselin noticed, as she, too, spent most of her time at the office.

Nelle and Grayson started meeting on Monday mornings via video call to synchronize their calendars for the week. Today was one of the rare occasions Nelle had enough free time to drive out to El Santo, while, as far as she knew, Grayson only had one appearance at a local craft beer festival on his schedule.

"Hi," Grayson said after kissing her until her legs forgot how to do their job. She clung to him, her arms entwined around his neck.

"Hi yourself." She pulled back to smile at him, but

it turned into a frown. "You look tired. Much more tired than you did on the call last night."

"You look gorgeous, as always. Although Face-Time never does justice to the color of your eyes." He smoothed a lock of hair off her face before growling in her ear, "It doesn't capture other things as well. Can't wait to see—and taste—those in person."

She laughed even as the promise in his voice made her shiver. "But you have to admit FaceTime makes phone sex far more interesting."

"Not a substitute for the real thing."

"No. Speaking of..." Her fingers traced the angle of his jaw, the curve of his lips. "When do we have to be at the festival and do we have time to start the in-person activities now?"

"Five o'clock, and sadly, no. Finley put a meeting with the county farm bureau on my schedule at the last minute. Which I have you to thank for."

"Me?" She laughed and allowed him to pick up her bag and then escort her to the house's vast main room, which held the kitchen, dining area and large living space. "How did I do that?"

"You asked me if I understood life in this district. So I asked her to set up meetings with the local associations and trade unions." He dropped her bag next to a sleek sofa that looked like it had just been delivered from a showroom and never been sat on. Then he drew her into his arms, tucking her tight against him. "I may have grown up here, but I have a lot to learn about the constituents."

She felt the rumble of his words almost more than

she heard them. She closed her eyes and nestled closer to his warm strength. "You'll get there."

He kissed her forehead and let her go. "Which means I need to leave. I'm sorry."

"No worries. We have tonight."

"We do." His phone rang. He looked at the screen, declined to answer and sighed. "I told them not to call unless it was an emergency. Yet it never stops ringing. Will you be okay here by yourself for a few hours?"

"Of course. I wish I could help you somehow, though."

"Knowing you're here, waiting for me, will help me more than you know. And unless you want to go over my personal receipts before I turn them into the campaign treasurer, there's not much else you can do."

"As a matter of fact, I probably can." This…whatever they were involved in…had come so out of the blue, there was a lot they still didn't know about each other's pasts. "I'm a certified financial planner. I've been known to look at receipts before."

Surprise creased Grayson's brow. "You are?"

"Well, I was. It's a long story. I'm happy to tell you if you want—"

His phone rang again. He declined the call with an annoyed gesture. "I do want. Tell me tonight?"

"I'd rather do other things with our time together, but sure."

His mouth twisted in a crooked smile. "I'm a good multitasker. In the meantime—if you want and you're not obligated—printouts of the campaign finance reports are on my desk, in the home office. Second door to the left off the hallway."

"Got it."

He picked up his keys and shoved them in his pocket before turning back to her. Taking her face in his hands, he traced the contours of her face with his gaze, lingering on her lips before looking into her eyes. "It's hard enough to hang up after our phone calls. It's hell to leave when you're here next to me."

"I'll still be here when you get back. In the flesh." She turned her head to kiss the palm of his hand where it cupped her cheek. "And maybe nothing else."

He groaned before crushing her mouth with his. "I'm canceling the beer festival appearance."

She lost herself once more in his kiss, until something hard vibrated against her. "I'd say you're happy to see me, but I'm pretty sure that's your phone again."

"Right on both accounts." He kissed her again, hard and fast. "See you in a few hours."

"Bye." She watched him as he left, then turned to take in her surroundings.

As far as rented houses in El Santo went, it was a very nice one. Similar in style but far larger than her childhood home. Something sparkling out the window caught her eye and she smirked. She hadn't grown up with a fully landscaped swimming pool in the backyard, either. The lots on her family's side of town were barely big enough for an inflatable wading pool.

Still, there were certain touches—the fireplace made of local stone, the still-wrapped gift basket on the counter containing nuts and dried fruits from nearby orchards—that were wholly El Santo. She wrapped her arms around herself. According to the old saying, you can't go home again, and she was more than fine with that. She'd not only shaken the dust off her shoes and left town, she'd thrown the shoes away. And until she met Grayson, she hadn't had any reason to return.

She ran her fingers over the smooth leather of the modern couch and noticed how her feet sank into the deep pile rug. She might have grown up in a place like this if Barrett hadn't betrayed her father, if her mother hadn't subsequently left him for someone with a steadier paycheck. But the thought didn't bring its usual resentment. Yes, what happened then was awful. Her father wasn't able to recover. But the past didn't need to continue to hurt her. She and Grayson could figure out the future.

Smiling, she set off down the hall toward Grayson's home office.

Two hours later, she was knee-deep in receipts, making notes for Grayson of any questions she had, when she heard a man clearing his throat. She looked up with a smile. "You're back! I didn't hear—"

She froze, her blood congealing somewhere around her ankles.

It wasn't Grayson standing before the desk as she expected.

It was his father.

"Hi," he said with an easy grin, holding out his

right hand for a handshake. "I'm Barrett Monk." She took his hand, her muscles acting on autopilot. Then he sat down in the overstuffed wing chair placed by the side of the desk. "You must be Nelle."

She nodded. She knew she should smile, speak. But she was frozen, her nerves encased in ice. She could only stare at him, her gaze fixated on the man whose name had haunted her growing up.

He was shorter than she anticipated. In her childish daydreams of revenge he had loomed over her, a monster of epic proportions. He was slight, too, for someone who'd taken his partner, one of the state's most promising litigation attorneys at the time, and broken him into pieces that couldn't be reassembled. But then his power lay not in brute strength but in his charisma, which hit her like a gust of wind from a winter storm. This was someone who got what he wanted because he made people gladly want to give it to him.

After what felt like an eternity but was probably more like ten seconds, she cleared her throat and forced her lips into a semblance of a smile. "Hello. Grayson's not here, but he should be back soon."

"Oh, I know." Barrett crossed one leg over the other and leaned back in his chair, as if he were an old friend stopping by to catch up. "I spoke to Finley before I headed over. She told me he was heading into a meeting with her and the farm folks. She also told me you were here."

He came here on purpose to see her? Nelle's stomach roiled. For a second she wondered if he was there to confront her about her father, but she dismissed it. Finley had said if she didn't know about the Lassen-Monk feud, then Barrett didn't care.

And Barrett's appearance wasn't a complete surprise. She'd been anticipating a meeting ever since Barrett's doctors gave him the all-clear last week to resume limited activities. She just wished Grayson was there.

Nelle made her smile bigger. "I hope this means you're feeling better."

"Eh, doctors." Barrett waved them off. "Bunch of old biddies, worried about the slightest blip and bloop. I'm going to live a good long time yet, don't you worry."

"I'm sure Grayson and Finley are happy to hear that." She straightened the keyboard on Grayson's desk so that it perfectly aligned with the edge of the desk, made sure all the pens had caps and were facing in the same direction. Anything to avoid being caught by Barrett's gaze. "I was about to get something to drink. Would you like something?"

"I'd like to talk to you. That's why I'm here, while my son and Finley are busy doing what they need to do."

"I—" Nelle began, but Barrett cut her off.

"Finley tells me you're doing a bang-up job for the campaign. You standing by Grayson's side has been a big help with the voters. I wanted to meet you and extend my thanks in person for your helpful contributions."

She blinked. Of the list of things she expected Barrett to say when they finally met face-to-face, this didn't make the top ten thousand. "But I'm not…"

She wasn't…what? Not acting the part for the campaign, but Grayson's actual girlfriend?

But was she? Really? He'd said he didn't want to go along with Finley's scheme. But on the other hand, they hadn't discussed their involvement beyond a vague "let's continue to see one another." They'd both been so busy. And when they did have limited precious time together, they were usually occupied with activities other than talking about their relationship.

She tucked a lock of hair behind her ear. "That's nice of Finley to say. Did Grayson agree?"

Barrett continued as if he didn't hear her. "The Cinderella thing is pure gold. Stroke of genius. My congratulations."

"I'm afraid that had nothing to do with me." Barrett's smile deepened. "You're modest. That speaks well for you. It's good to have you on the same page as us, Nelle."

The room was spinning, ever so slightly. "And what page is that?"

"The page where we all want Grayson to win, of course."

"I want Grayson to be happy," she countered.

Barrett chuckled. "Exactly. And for Grayson to be happy, he needs to fulfill the role he's prepared for his entire life. It's good to know you feel the same way, Nelle. I've got the feeling I can count on you. I can, right? Count on you?"

She finally looked him in the eye. His irises weren't the warm brown of Grayson's, but a dark, mesmerizing gray. His gaze pulled her in, as inescapable as gravity.

"Count on me for what?"

He spread his hands out and chuckled. "Why, just what we were talking about. Making Grayson happy by helping him win."

"I…he knows I'll help however I can. Whatever he thinks is best."

"Well, now, that's the thing. He doesn't really know what that is." Before she could interject, Barrett got out of his chair and walked to the front of the desk, placing his hands on the surface and leaning so they were face-to-face. "He may think he knows, but he's new to this game. I know, I know, he's a big deal up where you live, but around here, folks still think he's the kid who spends more time in the pool than on land."

"I don't think that's how voters see him—"

"I appreciate you defending my son. But I've been riding in this rodeo since before either of you was born. So can I count on you? This is Grayson's future happiness, after all."

Barrett's eyes twinkled with folksy charm, but hard-edged steel backed his words. She leaned back in her chair and crossed her arms over her chest. "Count on me for what?"

"Well now, you come to campaign events, you look

pretty…" He ran his gaze over her. "Which you do, but Finley should gussy you up more. You smile at the cameras. And when the campaign is over, you go home. By yourself."

Her pulse thudded in her ears. "By myself? I'm not sure I know what you mean—"

"Nelle, let me tell you something about men. We are simple creatures. We can either think with what God gave us between our shoulders or between our legs, but not both at the same time. Now, it's fine you two are having some fun at the moment. But when the election is over it will be pedal to the metal and my son will need to think with his brain."

"What makes you think he's not doing that now?" She held up her chin as she met the man's dark gray gaze head-on for the first time.

Barrett smiled, baring his teeth. It made her shiver. "You're a smart woman so I'm going to be straight with you. You're just fine for the campaign. I'm mighty thankful to have you on board."

"But?" Her heartbeat was almost deafening.

"But the Monks, well, we have a long, long legacy. Grayson's been raised to know his place. And when the election is over, Finley and I will find him a partner who can help him navigate Washington. He'll need one if he's going to succeed. And the more success he has, the happier he will be. We both agreed that's what we want for him." His gaze bored into hers.

"You're deciding what happiness looks like. I want him to decide that for himself."

Barrett leaned back in his chair. "I told you, he doesn't know enough yet to do that. But I think you do. Be honest, Nelle. Do you have what it takes to help my son be a successful congressman, heck, even president some day? To truly make him happy in the long run?"

She didn't answer. She'd be damned if she let Barrett see how many of her buttons he'd managed to push with exquisite precision. She focused instead on how Grayson's eyes lit up when he saw her, how he crushed her against him as if he never wanted to let her go. Their relationship, new as it was, did make him happy.

For now. The nagging voice in her head would not stop repeating the phrase on a loop.

In the silence, she heard the front door open. "Nelle? You still here? Ready for the festival?"

"In your office," she called, then stood up from the desk, knees trembling, and walked around it to face Barrett. "Good. We can ask him together about what he wants—"

But before she could finish, Grayson appeared in the doorway. "There you are…oh. Dad. I didn't know you were dropping by. How are you feeling? Do you need me?" Concern flooded his expression.

Barrett beamed at Grayson as if he and Nelle had been discussing the weather, nothing more. "I'm fine, son. Just feeling lonesome rattling around in that big house by myself now that the nurses have been dismissed. Finley mentioned the lovely Nelle was in town and I knew you were busy, so I asked my driver to bring me here in order to introduce myself. Hope you don't mind."

Grayson looked at Nelle, and she saw the apology in his expression. "Your doctors want you to take it easy, Dad. I was going to ask them if I could bring Nelle by your place tomorrow. This wasn't how I planned to introduce you to each other." He reached out and took Nelle's right hand, squeezing it gently.

She knew he was asking if she was okay. She gave him a reassuring squeeze back. "We had an interesting conversation. We both agreed we want you to find happiness."

Grayson's brows nearly hit his hairline. "Sounds very metaphysical and 'follow your bliss,' which isn't like either of you. But I'll take it."

"Speaking of, how would you define happin—"

"Why don't you get changed for the festival, Nelle," Barrett drowned out her words. "I overhead Finley saying she left some new clothes for you in the guest room closet. My voters sure do like a pretty girl in a dress."

"Nelle looks great as she is," Grayson said. "I love Radiohead."

Nelle looked down at her vintage band tour T-shirt and well-worn jeans, paired with sneakers. "I thought this would fit the craft beer vibe. But Finley has been having such a good time playing fairy godmother, I hate to disappoint her." She squeezed Grayson's hand one last time before leaving the room. But he wouldn't let her go.

"You don't need a different outfit," he said. "Dad,

do you want us to call your driver or should we drop you off on our way?"

"I'll take a ride, thank you, son. But before we go, there's one more thing I want to say to Nelle." Barrett folded his hands together in front of him. "Nelle, I am very sorry about what happened with your father."

Someone was breathing heavily in her ear. She gradually realized it was her, as her lungs strained to take in enough air. Grayson's palm was icy against hers. Or maybe the cold came from her own hand. She couldn't tell.

Grayson's gaze locked onto Nelle. "Dad? What do you mean?"

Barrett gave another of his expansive shrugs. "This happened before you were born, son. And you probably didn't hear the stories later because you were so busy with your practices and swim meets. But Nelle's dad got himself into some very hot water. Was even disbarred for stealing from clients. It was the talk of the town for a while." He turned to Nelle. "My big regret is I didn't do more to help him. We were friends in law school. We even thought about practicing law together. But your dad…he always did like the fine things in life a little too much. Taking off for the casinos as often as he did didn't help matters. Then your momma ran away. And if she couldn't change him… But I should have reached out, offered a hand. I always thought he resented me for not being a better friend, and y'know what? He was right. Please let Doug know I think of him often and wish him well. He's in Vegas now, if I'm not mistaken?"

Nelle stared at him, unblinking. Unmoving. That wasn't the story. Still, Barrett's description held some truths.

Her father did like to gamble and live beyond his means. Did he tell her his version so he wouldn't have to take responsibility for his own weaknesses? She could ask him, of course. But she knew what he would say. He never wavered in his telling of the tale, which was one of the reasons why she found it so convincing. His certainty fed hers. Now her world-view trembled, threatening to break into a thousand kaleidoscopic pieces as she struggled to take in Barrett's words.

Grayson's fingers stroked hers. At any other time, she would have welcomed his touch, leaning into it and returning it with caresses of her own. Now it felt like pity. She shook her hand free. "Yes, he moved to Las Vegas while I was in college. I'll give him your regards," she said, her words sounding as if they came from a distance.

"I'd appreciate that," Barrett said. "And I want you to know I do not hold your father's criminal actions against you. We are so proud to have an El Santo girl beside Grayson during the campaign."

"Dad—" Grayson warned, but Nelle cut him off.

"Look at the time," she said, pasting a bright smile on her face. "If I don't change now, we won't make it to the festival for your appearance." She had to get away. From both of them. She needed to think.

"We'll meet you out at the car," Barrett said. "We're going to have so much fun campaigning together, Janelle." His grin was back, as charming as before. But when his gaze caught hers, it was hard and opaque. "You don't mind if I use your full name, I hope? It just seems more you."

She fled the room.

Ten

Grayson rubbed his eyes and closed a window on his laptop. "That's enough for today," he told Finley.

Finley looked up from her own computer on the other side of the makeshift desk and frowned. "So soon?"

"It's almost ten. I'd like to get some sleep before I drive to Fremont in the morning." He yawned, then raised his arms over his head for a stretch. For once, they were alone in the campaign office. At best a stark and utilitarian space in the daylight, the rooms were even more nondescript at night without staffers and volunteers buzzing around the long folding tables and metal chairs. Campaign posters and flyers were tacked to the walls to add some color but the overall effect was still institutional beige, especially under the fluorescent lights. He took a doughnut from the pink box that had been sitting out since the day before, bit into it, made a face and threw the rest away. "Also, I need real food."

"You just want to call Nelle where I can't hear you." Finley continued to type on her laptop. "Which I'm all for, by the way. There are some things campaign managers don't need to know about their candidates' lives."

Nelle. He missed her. He wanted to be with her. In person, not on a video call.

But he was no longer certain she wanted to be with him. Something had intruded on the relationship they had been so carefully and steadily building. The problem had started when she came to El Santo to attend the beer festival three weeks ago.

He knew meeting his father hadn't been easy for her. Especially when Barrett explained the truth of his history with Nelle's father. But after her initial shock, she'd seemed to take it in stride. They'd had a great time together at the festival until she developed a killer headache. He'd done his best to nurse her through it, even though his contribution pretty much consisted of running a washcloth under cold water to put on her forehead and bringing her two aspirin. When they said goodbye the next morning, her kiss had ignited a blaze that still burned.

But ever since he watched her drive away, a barrier had sprung up between them. It wasn't high. It wasn't even that thick. But it was growing. It was almost imperceptible at first, but lately he brushed against it every time they spoke.

"Has Dad said anything to you about Nelle?" he asked.

Finley shook her head without looking at him. "Not really. He's happy she's from here. It's one more point in your favor for the voters."

The sugar in the doughnut made his empty stomach roil. Or maybe it was hearing Finley speak of Nelle as if she were an inanimate object, a mere bullet point on a presentation. He'd stated repeatedly that his relationship with Nelle had nothing to do with the campaign, and yet Finley continued to discuss her as if she were just another volunteer eager to help the cause.

"She's not a 'point,' as you put it. Or a campaign asset. I like her, Fin."

"Good." Finley kept her gaze on her screen. "She's the current girlfriend, so liking her works out well."

"I'm in love with her."

That got Finley's attention. Her gaze flew to meet his. "That's…great. Really great. She's a great person."

"I know I was scheduled to return tomorrow night, but I'm going to stay a few days longer in Fremont. I need you to clear my schedule."

She stared at him. "Why? I thought you were going for Nelle's work thing, whatever it is. And Barrett wants you to meet with Jon Wurtz while you're up there. His PAC was a major donor to Barrett's campaigns."

"Nelle's 'work thing,' as you put it, is a surprise lunch for her. She closed a four-million-dollar partnership with the Begaye Foundation." He shook his head. "No meetings. Clear means clear."

Finley pinched the bridge of her nose. "Okay. Don't meet Wurtz. But the debate is in two weeks. I need you to commit to the prep schedule."

"I've been prepping my entire life."

Finley shook her head so rapidly it was almost a blur. "That's not the same as prepping for this specific debate. Look, I get it, you're thirsty. Take a day, get it out of your system. But you need to take down your debate opponents and you're not there yet."

"It's not up for discussion." Grayson shoved his chair back, the metal legs scraping on the scarred linoleum floor. "I'm going to get some food and rest, then leave first thing in the morning."

Finley opened and closed her mouth a few times as if struggling with how to phrase her next words. That was a first for her in Grayson's experience. "If you have something to say, spit it out," he said.

Finley's sigh rang through the empty space. "Here's the deal. You're far ahead in the polls. So, yes, perhaps debate prep isn't the most pressing thing ever."

"Good. Talk to you in the morning." He turned to leave.

"But." The note in Finley's voice made him stop short. "The election is only the first hurdle. The easiest hurdle, in fact. If you win, you'll be moving to Washington for a good part of the year. And it's a twenty-four hour/seven days a week job. There's not a lot of downtime for…let's say, trips to Fremont. Which isn't even in your district."

Grayson regarded his sister. "You still haven't spit it out."

"I'm just saying you need to consider the effect winning will have on your life. And hers. You've known each other, what? Two months?"

"Longer."

"Not by much. Use that big brain of yours and think it through."

"I have."

Finley raised a skeptical eyebrow. "Sure, if you say so. But has Nelle?"

Irritation mixed with the stale sugar in his stomach. It was not a good combination. "A girlfriend for the campaign was your idea. Not mine."

"Yes, and I told you not to get serious. Date her, dump her."

"That's not happening."

"Then you and Nelle need to have a serious conversation."

He knew that. Finley's confirmation only renewed his determination to spend more time with Nelle. And figure out how to bring down the barrier for good.

He nodded. "We'll be fine." They had to be. He wouldn't accept anything else. "Clear my schedule for the next four days, okay?"

Finley's gaze searched his face. He kept his expression impassive. "I'll clear two days," she said. "If you commit to prep when you return."

"Three days." He bent down and kissed her on the top of her head. "Thanks."

"Just don't stink up the debate."

"I promise I won't." He looked over at her screen. "What are you working on?"

"Finishing today's emails. The accountants haven't heard back from Al on his review of the campaign finance report. Let me remind him he needs to sign it and then I can walk out with you." She started to type.

Grayson frowned. "Why haven't I seen the report?"

She glanced at him. "Al's the campaign treasurer, so he's in charge of signing and then filing it with the Federal Election Commission."

"Yes, thank you, I did pay attention when you explained campaign finances to me. But shouldn't I review it? I'm the candidate."

Her brow creased. "Do you want to review it? Barrett never did. Al was Barrett's treasurer for years. He'll let us know if he sees anything the FEC might object to. You have enough on your plate, especially since you're taking too many days off for a booty call."

Grayson ignored her last words. "Dad didn't have his own venture capital fund. I miss looking at numbers. Send it to me. I should be more familiar with the finances than I am, anyway."

"It's almost two hundred pages of names and dollar amounts. You sure you want to see it? We're coming up against the deadline to file for this quarter."

"You should've seen some of the business plans I used to receive. This sounds like light bedtime reading."

"Your eyeballs' funeral." She hit a key. "Sent. Let's get out of here."

Yoselin held her champagne flute out to clink it against Nelle's. "To you!"

Nelle laughed. "Shouldn't I be the one toasting you and Jason?" She nodded at the solitaire diamond winking on the fourth finger of Yoselin's left hand.

Yoselin held her hand out to admire her new ring. "It is pretty, isn't it? But this isn't about me." She took a sip and put her glass down. "Today is all about you, babe."

Nelle smiled. "It feels good to have a win, I have to admit." She looked around the private room of the elegant Indian restaurant. The table for twelve was set with a red cloth and china plates, and an elegant orchid arrangement in the center. A robin's-egg blue box tied with a satin bow occupied the far end of the table. "But you didn't need to do anything special."

"Oh, please, Octavia begged us to put this together. Oh, and she's insisting you call her Octavia now."

"Really?" Nelle's eyes widened. "That's not the champagne talking?"

"Bring in a major sponsor and you get special privileges." Yoselin winked at her. "She should be here soon."

"Who else is coming? People from the office?" But her question was answered when a man in a familiar Stetson entered the room. "Reid! What a terrific surprise."

"Hey, Nelle." He kissed her cheek and shook hands with Yoselin. "I wouldn't miss this. You're my favorite project we've promised to fund this year, and I'm not just saying that because I'm hoping to talk to your boyfriend when he shows up."

Nelle caught Yoselin's gaze. "Grayson is coming?"

She shrugged. "To see you accept a four-million check from an international foundation to help Bay Area children learn and thrive? Of course."

"Well, when you put it that way…" Nelle bit her lower lip. It was strange—a good strange! —to have so many things in her life headed in a positive direction at once. She kept waiting for the other shoe to drop. "But he's so busy. He's really taking the time off?"

At Yoselin's answering grin, something like a dam broke inside Nelle. A swell of happiness rose and crested, breaking down the wall of doubts that had crept higher and higher since her conversation with Barrett.

She hadn't seen Grayson in person since the beer festival, when she ended up sleeping in his guest room with a cold washcloth on her head to alleviate her migraine. They spoke every day, but his schedule was becoming tighter and tighter and the phone sex… well, that was still scorching hot and explosive. But then they would hang up and she would be back to wondering what, exactly, was her place in his life.

She knew he liked her. He'd told her that much. He might even like her a lot. But he liked a lot of people.

She, on the other hand, had zoomed past the point of no return long ago. She was in love with him. She'd fallen in love with his warm gaze and smart wit even when the rest of him was disguised as a clown. She fell deeper in love each time he held her, creating a world that was just the two of them. She was hopelessly in love with his kindness, his hundred different ways to be thoughtful.

Every time she allowed herself to hope that maybe, just maybe, this relationship didn't come with a hard expiration date, Barrett's words would echo in her head no matter how hard she tried to dismiss them.

It's okay to have fun now. But do you have what it takes to make him happy in the long run?

For the first time since that conversation, she dared to believe the answer might be yes.

"He did say he might be late, depending on traffic, and to start without him." Yoselin looked through the curtains that separated their room from the main restaurant. "And here's Octavia and the rest of the board of directors now." She waggled her eyebrows at Nelle. "Shall I tell our waiter to bring out the popadums?"

The wave of happiness kept Nelle buoyant throughout the various courses, from appetizers to *rasmalai* for dessert. But as the final plates were cleared and the last of the wine bottles were emptied, the seat next to hers remained empty. The wave receded, leaving her deflated and drained. It took all her energy to chat and laugh, to pretend nothing was wrong.

She smiled through the speeches and the toasts and the "a small token of our appreciation, really" presentation of the blue box. She smiled through the bestowing of the ceremonial check, with Reid demanding she come join him at the head of the table and accept a rectangle of cardboard that was almost too big to fit in the room. She smiled through the goodbyes, with Mrs. Allen—no, Octavia—telling her to take the rest of the day off. Finally, the room contained only her, Yoselin and a busboy clearing a few remaining dishes from the table. Her shoulders sagged.

Yoselin put her hand on Nelle's arm. "You okay?"

Nelle arranged her features into her most innocent expression. "Of course. Why wouldn't I be?"

"You know that wide-eyed thing doesn't work on me." Yoselin sighed. "I blame myself. I shouldn't have told you he was coming."

"I'm sure he got caught up in something to do with the election." She didn't sound convincing, even to her. "He'll call me when he can." She failed to mention that so far, her texts and messages had gone unanswered.

Yoselin folded her arms and regarded Nelle for a beat. "Be honest. You're not with him just because of Create4All, are you? As both your friend and your boss, if you're dating him for your job, don't."

"I'm not! I mean, yes, I met a lot of people through him who subsequently supported Create4All. But I'm not…that's not the reason we're…" How could she describe her relationship with Grayson when she didn't know their status? "Spending time together," she finished.

Yoselin gave her an assessing stare. "You sure?"

Nelle huffed. "If one of us is dating the other for their job, it's not me. He, on the other hand…" Argh. She pressed her lips together, to keep her thoughts bottled up so she couldn't voice them. They spilled out anyway. "For purposes of the election, he benefits from dating someone who grew up locally. And the whole Cinderella thing —" she waved a disgusted hand "—the media came up with after the gala plays really well with his voters."

"Are you fake-dating?" Yoselin's voice squeaked on the last word.

"No! At least, I'm not. And I didn't think he was. But then his father said…" She sighed. "My judgment feels broken."

Yoselin laid a gentle hand on her shoulder. "Your judgment works fine. Look at the ginormous check over there, and I'm not talking about the physical size of the cardboard. That was your work. I'm going to kick Grayson's ass for making you doubt yourself."

Nelle straightened up. She only had herself to blame for allowing Barrett's words to take up residence in her head. And maybe Barrett was right about her father being the unreliable narrator of his own story. She still hadn't received a straight answer from him.

But Grayson had never given her any reason to doubt his sincerity. To doubt the light in his eyes when he saw her. To doubt how he held her as if she held great value to him, the way his every gesture spoke of his thoughtfulness. The way they mutually ensured each other's pleasure.

She was falling into her old habits, she decided. Janelle would wring her hands and fret. That had been her reaction last year, when work turned into a disastrous nightmare. If she truly wanted to be New Nelle, to live her life as fully as possible, she had to stop being afraid and take action.

"If there are any asses to be kicked, it's mine. Can I have tomorrow off? I need to do what I should have done from the start."

She accomplished the drive to El Santo in less than three hours, thanks to minimal traffic and pushing her ten-year-old car as hard as she could. When she arrived at Grayson's rented house, she barely shut off the ignition before she was running up the path to the front door. She didn't concern herself with knocking, using the key he had given her the last time she visited and throwing open the heavy wood door. "Grayson!" she yelled into the echoing space. "We have to talk. Now."

Too late she realized he was probably at the campaign office. Or in a meeting with local officials. Or visiting a local school. Or at any other of the myriad places Finley had him running to and from, meeting voters and gathering donations. It had been a very dramatic plan, to burst into his house with a shouted demand, but the movie in her mind didn't contain any scenes past this one. Feeling slightly stupid, she turned to leave.

"Nelle?" Grayson emerged from the hallway that led to his office.

She bit back her gasp. He looked like hell. His eyes were bloodshot, his hair sticking up as if he had run his hands through it at frequent intervals, and his broad shoulders hunched as if trying to ward off a body blow.

She'd spent the entire drive building an impregnable stone fortress around her heart. One look at him and it crumbled. "What's wrong? Are you sick? Why didn't Finley call me?"

She'd never stopped to consider that something might have happened to him. Mostly because Grayson seemed so invulnerable, so impervious to the slings and arrows of life others encountered on a daily basis.

But she was wrong. So wrong. He was not invulnerable, but all too human. And she should have been the first to recognize that.

"Nelle. It is you." His gaze was alight with warmth and concern and, yes, caring. He held out his arms and she ran to him, throwing herself into his embrace. She wound her arms around his neck and buried her face in his shoulders, breathing in his scent. His clothes were rumpled, and a day's growth of beard darkened his jaw.

She ran her hand along the rough stubble, then lifted her head so she could kiss him. But he pulled back, keeping his arms around her but putting space between them. She frowned. "What's wrong?" she tried again.

Her earlier doubts tried to creep in. She shook them off. He might not love her, but there were feelings there. His grip wouldn't be so tight on her waist, as if she were the only life preserver in the middle of an ocean, if there weren't. "You're starting to scare me a little," she tried to joke.

He lifted his left hand to caress her cheek, as if to reassure himself it was really her. "It's so good to see you. But you shouldn't be—" He stopped. "But since you are, you can give me a second pair of eyes."

"Eyes for what?"

He let go of her then, his arms dropping to his sides. The gesture felt final. And that scared her a lot. "Come with me."

She followed him to his office and took the chair he offered behind his desk. Grayson took the wing chair to the side, his complexion gray despite the late afternoon sunlight streaming in from the windows. "I've highlighted the entries in question. You have a background in finance. Tell me what you see."

She glanced at the screen. The issue jumped out at her immediately.

"This doesn't make sense." She opened the calendar app on her phone. Maybe she had the date wrong…no. She was right. On the day in question, Grayson had been here, in El Santo. She knew because they had dinner plans in the Bay Area, but he had to cancel at the last minute when an opportunity to speak to a local women's club came up. So why was there a receipt for catering at one of San Francisco's most exclusive private clubs? A receipt for $4,462.34.

She glanced at some of the other highlighted entries. There was the $2,3780.45 spent at a pricey Los Angeles store that catered to celebrities, characterized as office supplies. But Grayson was adamant about not flashing his wealth around, choosing instead to purchase from local vendors. First-class plane tickets to San Diego had cost $1,200.28, and another $1,534.87 had gone to room charges at a pricey San Diego resort, supposedly to attend a fundraiser. But she and Grayson spoke every day. Maybe other people would fake being at home or in the office while gallivanting around the state, but not him. She knew that with every cell of her being.

She caught his gaze, feeling as shocked as he looked. Someone was using Grayson's campaign as their personal piggy bank. They weren't exorbitant amounts, but they added up. Whoever did this had not only cheated Grayson out of his funds but was committing a crime. Providing false information to the Federal Election Commission, which oversaw campaign financial records, could result in an investigation—and a lengthy jail term for fraud.

Was Finley responsible? As campaign manager she would have access to the campaign's credit card. But Nelle discarded her as the culprit almost immediately. Finley's methods might be over the top and personally intrusive, but she cared about her brother. She wouldn't jeopardize his reputation, not to mention his freedom.

Someone else, then. Someone who didn't think they would be caught. She looked up and held Grayson's gaze with hers. "I see the problem."

"So, not my imagination." Grayson rubbed his forehead.

"Do you know who's responsible?"

He didn't answer her.

"Grayson?"

He stirred, shaking his head as if to jar something loose. "You once called me a fair-haired prince. Or something like that."

She bit her lower lip. "Not my proudest moment, but yes."

"Growing up, I never questioned my place in the world. I accepted things were the way they were because that was how they were meant to be." A harsh chuckle escaped his lips.

"I think that's true for a lot of people," she said gently. "Especially those whose families provide them with a lot of advantages."

"I never thought to question why we lived in a big house. Or had private tutors. Or went on photo safari in Kenya over spring break."

"I wouldn't question a safari in Kenya. Sounds like fun." She tried to crack a smile.

"Maasai Mara. It's amazing. We should—anyway." He cleared his throat. "I believe you now. About your father's story."

"My father? You believe now that Barrett set him up?" She got up from the desk chair and came around to kneel at his feet, her arms folded on top of his knees. If only he would look at her. "Why now? What does this have to do with…" She stopped as an icy pit threatened to replace her stomach. "Wait. You don't think-—"

He nodded. "Barrett misappropriated the campaign funds."

"How do you know?"

"Because he stole not just from my campaign, but his. FEC filings are online. I looked up his previous records. They have the same issue. Dates and receipts don't match." Grayson met her gaze as he cupped her cheek in his right hand. "I'm sorry I missed your lunch. Is Yoselin mad at me?"

"I'd wear armor the next time you see her, but she'll get over it. Reid was there, too. He might have been the most disappointed to miss you." She kissed his palm, then stood up. "Right. So what do we do now?" She knew from painful experience that the sooner financial irregularities were rooted out and dealt with, the better.

His gaze turned as bleak as a landscape after a brush fire. "We break up."

Eleven

It was the hardest thing Grayson had ever done.

Harder than pulling the plug on a promising entrepreneur whose idea proved not to be viable after three years of trying. Harder than walking away from Monk Partners, an organization he'd built from the ground up with sweat, tears and countless late nights. Even harder than calling his father and confronting him with what the reports made clear. He didn't know if his heart would ever fully mend the deep, jagged hole torn in it by the look in Nelle's eyes after he said they had to break up.

But they were out of choices.

Nelle's chest rose and fell rapidly. "I don't understand. Why would you say that?"

He couldn't look at her. He shouldn't have looked

at her in the first place. One glance and he was intensely aware of her full lips that fit against his as if custom-crafted for that purpose. Of her crystal-blue gaze, begging him to tell her he was joking or mistaken. Her lush curves, warm and soft and delectable, a treasure-laden territory he would never tire of exploring.

The way she made him laugh. And challenged him to be a better person. In a way, if he hadn't met Nelle, he wouldn't have the strength to do what he had to do. He had to let her go.

His family had hurt hers. He knew that now. He would never stop kicking himself for doubting her story, for accepting his father's glib twisting of the truth. It was also made plain to him his family would continue to hurt her if she remained in their orbit. He had the opportunity to stop the cycle.

He pressed hard on the spot between his eyebrows where the headache had persisted since the early hours of the morning. "I called Barrett this morning, as soon as I knew he would be awake."

He heard her sharp inhale. "And?"

"He didn't deny it. He laughed. Congratulated me, even. Said he knew I was smart."

She slipped her hand into his. He didn't want to be reminded of her touch. They should make a clean break. But he twined his fingers with hers. One last time, to store the memory of her silken skin sliding against his, the warm strength of her fingers ironically lending him the courage to do what he must. "He and Al, the treasurer, have been conspiring for years to use the campaign funds as their personal checking account. They've been careful to keep the expenses just unremarkable enough that they don't draw greater attention. And that's how he took me diving on the Great Barrier Reef for my sixteenth birthday. He wrote it off as visiting a US naval station in the South Pacific."

"Here in El Santo, everyone thought your family was…"

"Rich? So did I." He sighed. The adrenaline that had kept him going for eighteen hours straight was starting to dwindle. "I discovered Dad lost the fortune he inherited before I was born. He invested it in a Ponzi scheme. And to get the money back, he stole from his law practice—"

"And framed my father." Her hand was cold in his.

"I'm so sorry I didn't believe you." And he was. More than he could ever put into words.

She took in a shuddering breath. "Okay. So now we both know the truth. But why did you say we have to break up?"

He let go of her hand and came around the desk to take the chair she had vacated. He sat down and opened a new set of files. "Barrett emailed this while I was on the phone with him."

She stood behind him and peered over his shoulder. "What the—oh. No. Oh no."

He turned and got up in time to grab her elbow as she wobbled. "Don't faint."

Her glare could turn sweet cream into sour. "I

tripped over the rug. I'm not going to faint. I'm going to kick—"

"My father's ass? Get in line. But there's a problem—he's in the hospital."

Nelle gasped. "What?"

"Finley found him prostrate on the floor after we hung up. The doctors at the hospital said his life isn't in danger, but they're admitting him for the duration. He's undergoing tests now." Grayson had been heading for the shower to clean up before joining his sister in the waiting room when Nelle appeared. As if things weren't awful enough, he'd almost added causing his father's fatal attack to the list of the day's events.

"I wish him a fast recovery."

He ran a hand through his hair. "Yeah, well, I'd understand if you didn't."

"He's still your father." Nelle's gaze searched his. "You can dislike the person your father is but still love him."

"What if I had killed him?" The thought would forever haunt him.

Steel entered Nelle's gaze. "He brought this on himself. He took money that didn't belong to him. You have nothing to do with it."

He shook his head. "I can't turn and walk away from this family. But you can. You must. If not, Barrett will hold this—" he pointed at the computer screen "—against you. I can't let that happen."

Nelle looked back at the files open on the screen. There it was, in black-and-white plus a few color photos. Her life in New York City, well curated to show only the worst. A photo from a birthday dinner, after a few bottles of champagne with friends. She was half draped over a former boyfriend, her dress riding up and exposing her thighs, her eyes glazed from drinking. The ledger of the accounts her co-worker had doctored in order to sabotage her chances of receiving the promotion they were both pursuing. The letter terminating her employment. There was even the denial from the New York State unemployment office because she had been let go for work-related misconduct.

She pressed her lips together. Her past wasn't a secret. But it also wasn't something she volunteered. She pulled her sweater tighter around her, as if it could provide some of the privacy that had been stripped from her. "I never said I was perfect. But nobody's perfect. People make mistakes. That's why the human race was given the ability to forgive."

"There's nothing here to forgive. I know your co-worker orchestrated the whole thing. Yoselin told me."

"You knew?"

"I was waiting for you to tell me. I figured it would take time before you felt safe enough to trust me. I wanted to give you that time."

"I was going to tell you the night of the beer festival, but then…" She ran a hand through her hair. "I guess… I'll always be embarrassed the same thing happened to both my father and to me." She laughed, even though nothing felt like it would ever be humorous again. "Harry—that's my co-worker—probably got the idea from listening to me talk about my dad as a cautionary tale. How's that for irony?"

She turned back to the screen. "I'm surprised the media didn't dig this up first."

"Barrett bought their silence. For the length of the campaign."

Her mouth fell open, but she was too frozen with shock to form words.

Grayson continued, his tone bleak. "And if the campaign finance fraud becomes public, Barrett will put the blame on you."

That unfroze her. "What? How? I don't have access to the campaign funds."

"You helped with my personal accounts."

She did. It was the day she met Barrett. Right in this office.

"You've had access to my computer. So you had an opportunity to steal the credit card credentials."

Nelle's breath caught in her throat. All it would take would be a few well-placed whispers and the media would spin a story, using her history in New York City. Then bring in her dad's history. The financial fraudster daughter of a criminal embezzler.

"I told you the past was past and it didn't shape the present. I was wrong." Grayson closed the files and turned to face her. "But I'm stopping the cycle. For you."

For her? Flashes of red appeared in Nelle's vision. "Oh, no. You're not doing this. You're not playing the noble martyr. Especially not for me. I don't need saving and even if I did, I can save myself."

He drew himself up to his full height. "It's not under your control. This is my family, my problem, and it has to be my solution. You'll be hurt otherwise."

"But you *are* hurting me. This, what you're doing right now, hurts like hell. I love you, damn it! I've loved you since you handed me a warm, watered down drink." She held out her right hand. "Please. We can figure this out. Together. The past can only affect us if we let it."

So many conflicting emotions flew across his expression she couldn't keep track of them all. His gaze lifted to meet hers. The glowing gold shards in his eyes made them appear lit from within. Her heart beat in triple time as he lifted his hand to meet hers. "Nelle, I—"

His phone rang. He dropped his hand and the moment fled, as if it had never existed. He turned away from her and looked at the screen, then answered it with a curt "Yes?" He walked to a far corner of the room and spoke into the receiver in a hushed whisper.

She watched him, pretty sure her heart was in her eyes. And in her lungs. And in her stomach. Her entire body pulsed, waiting for him to finish his conversation and return to her.

But when he did, the look on his face caused her heart to fall into her shoes. And stay there. "That was Dad. He's awake and wants to see me."

"I'll come with you."

He screwed his eyes shut. When he opened them, the light they had possessed was gone. "I'm ahead in the polls. Barring a disaster, the election is as good as won. I'll be moving to Washington, which means our relationship would be at an end regardless. It just came sooner than expected."

He would not meet her gaze. "I love you," she said again. "And I think you care for me."

"I have to go." He shoved his laptop into a leather bag. "Thanks for your help. I wish you all the very best. Always."

She ran ahead of him and blocked the doorway so he couldn't exit the room. "You told me in Napa after our first night together that it meant something to you. That I mean something to you. Look me in the eye and tell me those were all lies."

He stood very still. Then he lifted his head. His whiskey brown gaze burned hot with pain and regret, searing her heart. "I'm sorry."

The world faded to a pinprick as oceans roared in her ears. She leaned on the doorjamb for support, allowing room for Grayson to pass before she could process what was happening. He didn't mean it. He wasn't really going through with the breakup. She ran after him as soon as her muscles unfroze enough to move. "Grayson—"

The sound of the front door shutting and his car starting in the driveway was the only response she received.

This couldn't be the end. He was exhausted and in shock. His emotions were at the breaking point. In a few hours, when he had more information about Barrett's health, he would see things differently. There was too much between them for him to walk away. Too much that was real. She could wait.

And wait.

And wait some more.

When morning rolled around and Grayson still hadn't returned to his house nor answered any of her calls or texts, she got in her car and drove back to Fremont.

"And in the race for California's fifty-fourth district, Silicon Valley venture capitalist Grayson Monk is far out in front of the pack to fill his father's congressional seat in the upcoming special election. The debate this evening is seen as just a formality. Former congressman Barrett Monk is still in the hospital recovering from—"

Nelle turned off the television, a giant fist squeezing her heart into spiky shards. Even in her new apartment, with zero things in it to remind her of Grayson, he still managed to be present. She told herself it would take more time. Two weeks wasn't nearly long enough to heal her gaping wounds. Although, who was she kidding. She would never fully be over him at the rate she was going.

Her phone rang. The screen read, "No Caller ID." She answered anyway. Living by herself was a bigger adjustment than she'd anticipated. Even a computer-generated voice telling her she'd won an all-expenses-paid trip if she would just provide a credit card number would be a welcome break in the silence. "Hello?"

It wasn't a computerized voice. Nelle almost dropped the phone in surprise, but not before she heard Finley ask, "Where are you?"

"What do you mean, where am I?"

"You're not here, which means you have to be somewhere. When will you get here?"

Nelle sank down on the secondhand couch Octavia had insisted on giving her. "Get where?"

She could practically hear Finley's eyes roll. "El Santo. The debate is tonight." Her tone implied a "duh" at the end.

Nelle burst out laughing. She liked Finley a lot, but her tolerance of the other woman's audacity had its limits. "How about never? Is that a good time to arrive?"

"That isn't funny," Finley snapped. "This is the debate. It's a big deal as we head toward election day. And did you or did you not promise me you would show up for the *entire* campaign?"

Nelle stared at her phone in disbelief. Finley couldn't be serious. Could she? Nelle slammed the phone back against her ear. "Your brother and I are not involved anymore. He said goodbye."

"Yes, well, I don't care. Sleep with him, don't sleep with him, that's between you two. But I'm in charge of the campaign, not him. And you promised *me*. He had no power to release you from that promise."

Nelle didn't know whether to laugh or cry. "I can't. You have to understand why. Somewhere under your shark suit is a human."

"Clever." Finley's tone implied it was anything but.

Then she sighed, and the snap in her tone softened. "Look, I know this family is a lot. I know Barrett is a master manipulator who can make you swear on a stack of Bibles that the sky is chartreuse and the grass is fuchsia."

"And a thief and a fraudster. When are you turning him in to the Federal Elections Commission?"

"Who says we haven't? Not everything is on the internet. The real question is why haven't *you* turned him in?"

Nelle shut her eyes. It was true. She hadn't called the FEC. Despite the finality of Grayson's goodbye, she would never do anything that might harm him or his chances of success. "I'm going to hang up now."

Finley huffed. "Fine, don't come. But if you don't, I'll let the FEC know you had material evidence about campaign finance fraud and didn't tell them. So, talk to you later—"

"Wait!" Nelle ran through what she knew of FEC regulations in her head. "I don't think that's a thing. Is it?"

"There's one way to find out. If you don't come to the debate, that is."

"This is blackmail, Finley."

"No, it's enforcement of a verbal contract between two parties. So. You coming?"

Nelle looked down at her outfit. She was wearing her oldest pair of jeans, topped by vintage Pearl Jam T-shirt. "It would take me at least an hour to get ready, and then three hours of driving. By the time

I get there, the debate will be long over. You can't blackmail the laws of physics into obeying you."

"Don't you know me by now? Go downstairs. Take your purse and lock your door."

She should say no. She should have ended the call as soon as she knew it was Finley, for that matter. But she left her apartment and went downstairs to her building's front entrance. Her curiosity would never forgive her otherwise.

She burst out laughing when she opened the door and saw what awaited her. "Nice one," she said into the phone.

A man in a military-style pilot jumpsuit wearing aviator sunglasses was standing by a large Mercedes sedan. "CC's Helicopter Tours" read the magnetic sign affixed to the side of the vehicle. "Ma'am," the man said, giving her a salute. "Ready to go to the airport?"

"Laws of physics solved," Finley said. "The helicopter will get you here in time. See you soon." The phone disconnected.

"Ma'am?" The man opened the rear passenger door.

Nelle shook her head. "I don't think so. But please tell Finley she gets an A for effort—" She stopped. What was on the rear seat? Was that…?

It was. An aqua and silver dress. Not her ballgown from the gala; this one was more appropriate for day wear. But it had a full skirt and silvery-pearl buttons on the bodice.

A note was attached. "Courtesy of your friendly

neighborhood fairy godmother," it read on one side. And on the reverse: "I never beg but I'm begging now. Please come to the debate. I know he messed up but he needs you. And then I promise you never have to see any of us again if you don't want to."

The man cleared his throat. "Excuse me, but the copter is waiting."

Nelle took a deep breath. Her soul was still raw and bleeding from Grayson's goodbye. She didn't owe him or Finley a thing. By every right, she should march back into her apartment and put her phone on silent. She had tried being New Nelle. She had tried going after what she wanted. She had failed. And it still hurt.

Her gaze fell on the note. *He needs you.*

She entered the sedan, sat down and buckled the seatbelt.

Twelve

Grayson glanced in the mirror of the dressing room assigned to him for the debate. It was being held in the local community college's auditorium and apparently the last occupants of this room had worn some sort of costume made of feathers, because yellow and purple and orange ones were everywhere. He straightened his tie, then decided he didn't like the knot and undid it. He'd just finished tying a new knot when Finley walked in.

"How are you doing?" Her usually precise haircut was a touch shaggy, and her tailored suit hung off her frame instead of being fitted to her contours. However, for the first time in days, a hint of her usual spark was back in her gaze.

"I could ask the same of you."

"Doesn't matter how I feel. You're the main event." Finley brushed at the shoulders of Grayson's jacket. He allowed her ministrations, knowing it was as much a nervous tic of hers as it was ensuring his suit was lint-free.

"I'm fine." And he was. For the first time in a long time—since he found Finley trying to make coffee that morning in his penthouse in San Francisco—he was utterly calm, cool and collected. "Don't worry."

"I'm not," she said. But she wouldn't look him in the eye. If he didn't know better, he'd think she was hiding something from him. "I'm looking forward to this debate being over, however. You're going to kick ass."

"I know." He also knew by the time the night was through, Finley might be looking to kick his ass. He took a deep breath. "Fin, why aren't you the one running?"

"What?" This finally got her to look up. "What are you talking about?"

"Why aren't you the one running for this seat? You know the district. You know Washington. You know the job, inside and out. You'd be an amazing congresswoman."

Finley chuckled. "Jokes to loosen up before you go on stage. That's a good tactic."

"I'm not joking. Why aren't you Barrett's heir apparent?" He grabbed her hands and kept them still in his.

She laughed again, but this time there was no mirth in the sound. "You know why. Barrett may be the only father I know, but I'm not his blood. There's only one heir, apparent or otherwise, in this family."

"It should be you. You should be the one going on this stage."

Finley snatched her hands away. "Let's go over your position on farm subsidies again. You promise to…" She lifted her eyebrows. "C'mon, fill in the rest."

He shook his head. "I'm sorry for being so blind."

She huffed. "That's a terrible answer, especially when your toughest competition is a rancher who knows subsidies inside and out. Try again."

"I'm sorry I didn't pay attention to how Barrett treats you. He constantly takes but never gives."

For a second, Finley's air of amused superiority slipped. Then a knock came at the door, and a production assistant ducked his head in to let them know Grayson had ten minutes to get to the stage. She lifted her chin and smirked at him, the armor back and wrapped even thicker around her. "All I know is you're about to go on that stage and show the people of this district their next congressman. Break two legs and an elbow."

He hugged her. Finley stiffened, her arms hanging at her side, before tentatively returning the hug. They weren't a demonstrative family. He couldn't recall the last time Barrett showed fatherly affection. Maybe not since their mother died. But that was going to change. Finley deserved her full place at the family table. And she would get it. He'd make sure of that. "Thanks, sis. For everything. Your faith in me has meant a lot."

Finley's cheeks were bright red, but she waved off his words. "You sound as if you're about to leave on a trip to Mars. It's just an hour's debate. Get out there."

He nodded. "Right." He took a quick glance in the mirror, straightened his tie and opened the door. Oddly, he wasn't nervous. The speech at the gala had caused him more apprehension, even though the stakes tonight were much higher. Clarity of purpose was a terrific antidote to nerves. One last check of his inside suit jacket pocket, ensuring its contents were still there, and he was ready to go on stage. "See you on the other side."

Nelle arrived at the auditorium just as the outer doors were being closed and no more audience members were allowed in. She had to wave her backstage pass at a grumpy attendant or she would have been left out on the sidewalk with the other latecomers. She pushed open the door to the main auditorium to the sound of recorded horns and brass playing patriotic-sounding riffs. Too late to go backstage, she looked around for an empty seat. The only one she spotted was in the middle of a row, which meant she had to climb over purses and backpacks while trying and failing to avoid stepping on toes to reach it.

The stage was brightly lit, illuminating the black curtain backdrop and the podiums draped with red, white and blue bunting. The debate moderators sat at a long table set up before the stage, two cameras from the local television station flanking them as they faced where the candidates would stand. Nelle's palms were wet, but she didn't want to wipe them on the delicate fabric of the aqua and silver dress.

The helicopter got her to El Santo with an hour to spare to change into her new finery. Finley had thoughtfully also provided make-up, hairstyling tools and silver sandals with stiletto heels. However, Nelle's hands had shaken so much, she used up most of time putting on and then taking off lipstick and mascara.

The lights in the audience dimmed. The music changed to a fanfare. A disembodied voice began the night's announcements.

And there he was.

Her heart constricted as Grayson waved and smiled at the audience. Really, no one should be that handsome. Or maybe he was so attractive because it came from his inner self, not just the accident of genes that led to the symmetry of his facial features.

She leaned forward, her pulse beating so loud in her ears she could barely comprehend what was being said, despite the excellent acoustics and expertly mixed sound system. Other candidates joined him on stage, but she barely noticed them. Her entire focus was captured by him.

Too late, she joined in the applause after the field was introduced. Then the audience settled, a hush descending upon the auditorium as the debate moderators began to explain the procedure for the evening and the rules they would be following.

Nelle closed her eyes. She just had to survive the debate. She wasn't sure why Finley said he needed her as Grayson looked just fine. More than fine. Thriving. Certainly not as if he'd spent the last two weeks pining for her.

Next time, she would not answer the phone. No matter what name was on the screen.

"Next, let's hear from Grayson Monk. Mr. Monk?"

The moderator's voice cut through what little Zen Nelle had achieved. Her gaze flew to Grayson, tall and lean and exuding calm confidence. He took the microphone from its stand. "Mind if I step out from behind the podium?" When the moderator gave his assent, Grayson moved downstage. "I know the question is about my position on the national defense budget. But I'd like to beg the audience's—and my opponents'—indulgence for a minute."

The audience around her started to murmur as Grayson stepped to the edge of the stage. Both cameramen focused their lenses on him. "It has been a privilege coming back to El Santo. You have all taught me so much. When I began this campaign, I thought being your representative was what I was meant to do. It was what I was raised for, growing up as Barrett Monk's son—to carry on the legacy of public service that began with my great-grandfather, who was governor of this state."

On the stage his opponents were starting to shuffle their feet, their expressions ranging from confused to annoyed. "This is highly irregular—" a former city council member started to say.

Grayson turned to him. "You're right. I'll be brief." He faced the audience again. "But what I learned as I got deeper into the campaign is you don't need someone with a family name or a legacy as your representative. You need a representative who is deeply involved with this district and its people, who has been here, fighting the good fight alongside you. You all taught me I have so much more left to learn about El Santo, its resources and its people. Your hopes and your dreams, your past and your future." He stopped and cleared his throat. Nelle edged forward until she almost fell off her seat, her bottom lip numb from biting it so hard.

"Someday I might stand before you and ask you to vote for me. But now is not the time." He paused to raise his right hand, cutting the glare from the bright lights shining in his face. He looked down at someone in the front row, his gaze laser-focused. "To paraphrase someone I care about very much, you deserve a representative who will put you, the voters of this district, first. Not their family name, not their power over others, not their appearance. The masks need to come off."

Nelle inhaled, a sharp, audible gasp. The people seated next to her turned to glare in her direction.

Then Grayson swung his gaze up to sweep the entirety of the auditorium. "I'm withdrawing from the race and taking my name off the ballot. You have great candidates up here, and I urge you to vote for the person you feel will do the best job of taking your voice to Washington. As for me, I'm going to find the woman who wore this mask and spend the rest of my life making up to her for taking two weeks to figure out what really matters. Thank you."

And he pulled out an aqua-blue mask decorated with seashells and crystals and faux pearls.

The auditorium spun around Nelle as the crowd erupted into a cacophony of noise. The lights, the decibels of sound, the heat of a room filled to capacity with people packed into tight rows: her senses couldn't keep up. Only two things cut through the overload: one, he had her mask. The one she thought lost forever on a San Francisco street. She struggled to breathe. It was as if her ribcage was too small to contain her heart.

He did care. From the moment they met. That kiss the night of the gala was as special to him as it was to her.

And two: Grayson was giving up his dream. For her. A dream that would also benefit others, as he would be a damn fine congressman. Did Finley know he was going to do this? Is that why she wanted Nelle here, to stop him? "You can't step down!" She was on her feet and climbing over the people in her row, heedless of stepped-on toes, before she had time to think through her actions. She flew down the aisle toward the stage. One of her stiletto heels caught on the carpet and she stopped herself from falling just at the last minute. She kicked off the sandals to regain her speed. "You have to stay in the race."

Too late, she realized she had drawn the attention off Grayson and onto herself. One of the cameras swung to focus on her, while the other remained on him. She glanced to her left and then to her right and saw hundreds of pairs of eyes staring back at her. She stood still, her chest heaving. "Don't do it," she said in a quieter voice.

"Nelle?" Grayson still shielded his eyes, trying to find her in the auditorium.

"Yes," she said, her gaze seeing him and him only. Then hands were at her elbows and she was being helped onto the stage, guided forward until she stood facing him. She instinctively reached out to touch him, but when the audience started to "ooh" and "aah" she pulled back and gave him a half wave instead. "Um, hi."

"Hi yourself," he said. He looked around. She followed his gaze. His former opponents exhibited various stages of shock, some leaning on their podiums with wide gazes and open mouths, others frantically texting on their phones. The moderators shuffled though their scripts while the camera operators spoke intently into their headpieces, keeping the lenses focused on Nelle and Grayson. He took off his lapel mike, tossing it aside so they wouldn't be overheard. "I thought you didn't like big crowds," he said with a lopsided grin.

"I don't. But this is too important to let a fear of crowds get in the way." She shook her head. "I mean it. Don't drop out. Not for me. This is all you've wanted. This is your dream—"

He tucked a loose strand of hair behind her ear. "It's not. It's what other people dreamed for me."

"But you worked toward this your entire life. Your education, running the fund—"

"Only because I thought I had to be the person I was supposed to be."

"Right. And you can't give that up. Especially not for me."

He smiled and cupped her face with his hands. "Nelle, darling Nelle. Will you believe the truth? I'm not doing this for you."

She narrowed her gaze. "You broke up with me for my own good."

"And that is unforgivable. But then I remembered something a very wise woman said to me. About doing the right thing versus the supposed thing."

Nelle rolled her eyes. "Oh. Her. She's a bit of a know-it-all."

"Hey, don't talk that way about the love of my life." His expression turned sober. "Running for office, protecting my dad because he threatened you to hurt you if I didn't—those were things I was supposed to do. It's time to do the right thing."

"But are you sure pulling out of the race is the right thing?"

"It should have been Finley in the first place. Not me. Politics are her passion, not mine."

"Oh?" Nelle's shock was wearing off, replaced by a warm, fizzing sensation she could only identify as joy. "And what are you passionate about?"

He glanced up at the crowded auditorium, then bent down so his mouth was by her ear. "Ask me in an hour when I have you naked in my bed and I'll show you."

She shivered at the promise in his tone. "By all means, follow your passion."

He grinned. "Believe me, I fully intend to explore it." Then his smile faded. "But we should stop by the hospital to see how Barrett took my announcement first."

She took a deep breath. "Of course."

"He knows he's going to be indicted. The FEC is investigating as we speak." Grayson straightened up. "He's still my father, though."

"I know."

"It might be a rough few years as the case winds through the courts."

She nodded. "You'll get through them. You and Finley both. Speaking of Finley, where is she?" Her gaze searched for Grayson's sister in the sea of TV cameramen, assistants, candidates, and the occasional audience member who had wandered out of their seat. It was clear the debate's producers hadn't made a decision yet whether to go forward with the remaining candidates or cancel.

"Not sure. My guess is she had the same concern as me and went to visit Dad. She knew he'd be watching the debate on television."

"I hope he's okay with your decision."

"He doesn't get a say. Especially since after his latest heart episode he gave me power of attorney over his estate." Grayson cupped her cheek with his left hand. "That's one of the reasons why it's taken this long to withdraw from the race. I needed to secure the power of attorney first. We're going to liquidate his assets. The proceeds will go to schools and social services in this district."

"Grayson," she breathed.

"The money rightfully belongs to them anyway. I made more than enough with Monk Partners to take care of him for the rest of his life. I'd like to set up a pension for your father, too. If that's okay with you."

She nodded, her heart too full to form words.

"And speaking of rest of one's life…" He dropped to one knee.

The background auditorium noise, humming steadily since Grayson made his announcement, tripled in decibels. Cameras appeared as if by magic, pointing at the two of them. And then Nelle could only see and hear the man in front of her, holding out a familiar mask.

"Once upon a midnight, masked strangers shared a kiss and I fell in love. Now that I know you, Nelle Lassen, that love only grows stronger and deeper every hour. I can't imagine spending another minute without you by my side. Will you marry me?"

She heard music. Maybe it came from the auditorium speakers, maybe it was angels singing hallelujah, or maybe it was just her heart, a song of joy so overwhelming it filled her ears. She shook as he reached for her hand and placed the mask in it. "Yes! I love you, Grayson." She smiled at him, even as tears fell down her cheeks. "And I can't wait to write our future story. Together."

He kissed her then, in front of the other candidates and the cameras and crowd. A chorus of *awww*s rose from the audience, ringing in her ears. Then his kiss deepened, and he pulled her tight against him, his hands tangling in her hair, and the world narrowed to just the two of them. The mask dangled off the fourth finger of her left hand.

* * * * *

*If you loved
Nelle and Grayson,
don't miss
Luke and Danica's story
Wanted: Billionaire's Wife
by Susannah Erwin.*

*Available exclusively from
Harlequin Desire.*

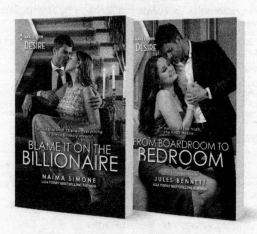

SPECIAL EXCERPT FROM

(H)HARLEQUIN

DESIRE

*Billionaire Anderson Stone doesn't deserve
Piper Blackburn, especially after serving time in prison.
But now he's back, still wanting the woman he can't
have. Could her faith in him lead to redemption
and a chance at love?*

Read on for a sneak peek at
The Rebel's Redemption *by Kira Sinclair*

He had no idea what he was doing. But that didn't matter. The millisecond the warmth of her mouth touched his, nothing else mattered.

Like it ever could.

The flat of his palm slapped against the door beside her head. Piper's leg wrapped high across his hip. Her fingers gripped his shoulders, pulling her body tighter against him.

He'd never wanted to devour anything or anyone as much as he wanted Piper.

Her lips parted beneath his, giving him the access he desperately craved. The taste of her, sweet with a dark hint of coffee, flashed through him. And he wanted more.

One taste would never be enough.

That thought was clear, even as everything else in the world faded to nothing. Stone didn't care where they were. Who was close. Or what was going on around them. All that mattered was Piper and the way she was melting against him.

His fingers tangled in her hair. Stone tilted her head so he could get more of her. Their tongues tangled together in a dance that was years late. Her nails curled into his skin, digging in and leaving stinging half-moons. But her tiny breathy pants made the bite insignificant.

He needed more of her.

Reaching between them, Stone began to pop the buttons on her blouse. One, two, three. The backs of his fingers brushed against her silky, soft skin, driving the need inside him higher.

Pulling back, Stone wanted to see her. He'd been fantasizing about this moment for so long. He didn't want to miss a single second of it.

Piper's head dropped back against the wall. She watched him, her gaze pulsing with the same heat burning him from the inside out.

But instead of letting him finish the buttons, her hand curled around his, stopping him.

The tip of her pink tongue swept across her parted lips, plump and swollen from the force of their kiss. Moisture glistened. He leaned forward to swipe his own tongue across her mouth, to taste her once more.

But her softly whispered words stopped him. "Let me go."

Immediately, Stone dropped his hands and took several steps away.

Conflicting needs churned inside him. No part of him would consider pushing when she'd been clear that she didn't want his touch. But the pink flush of passion across her skin and the glitter of need in her eyes… He felt the same echo throbbing deep inside.

"I'm sorry."

"You seem to be saying that a lot, Stone," she murmured.

"I shouldn't have done that." He felt the need to say the words, even though they felt wrong. Everything inside him was screaming that he should have kissed her. Should have done it a hell of a long time ago.

Touching her, tasting her, wanting her was right. The most right thing he'd ever done.

But it wasn't.

Piper deserved so much more than he could ever give her.

Don't miss what happens next in…
The Rebel's Redemption *by Kira Sinclair.*
Available September 2020 wherever
Harlequin Desire books and ebooks are sold.

Harlequin.com

HDEXP0820

Get 4 FREE REWARDS!

We'll send you 2 FREE Books plus 2 FREE Mystery Gifts.

Harlequin Desire® books transport you to the world of the American elite with juicy plot twists, delicious sensuality and intriguing scandal.

FREE Value Over $20

YES! Please send me 2 FREE Harlequin Desire novels and my 2 FREE gifts (gifts are worth about $10 retail). After receiving them, if I don't wish to receive any more books, I can return the shipping statement marked "cancel." If I don't cancel, I will receive 6 brand-new novels every month and be billed just $4.55 per book in the U.S. or $5.24 per book in Canada. That's a savings of at least 13% off the cover price! It's quite a bargain! Shipping and handling is just 50¢ per book in the U.S. and $1.25 per book in Canada.* I understand that accepting the 2 free books and gifts places me under no obligation to buy anything. I can always return a shipment and cancel at any time. The free books and gifts are mine to keep no matter what I decide.

225/326 HDN GNND

Name (please print)

Address   Apt. #

City   State/Province   Zip/Postal Code

Email: Please check this box ☐ if you would like to receive newsletters and promotional emails from Harlequin Enterprises ULC and its affiliates. You can unsubscribe anytime.

> Mail to the **Reader Service:**
> **IN U.S.A.:** P.O. Box 1341, Buffalo, NY 14240-8531
> **IN CANADA:** P.O. Box 603, Fort Erie, Ontario L2A 5X3

Want to try 2 free books from another series? Call 1-800-873-8635 or visit www.ReaderService.com.

*Terms and prices subject to change without notice. Prices do not include sales taxes, which will be charged (if applicable) based on your state or country of residence. Canadian residents will be charged applicable taxes. Offer not valid in Quebec. This offer is limited to one order per household. Books received may not be as shown. Not valid for current subscribers to Harlequin Desire books. All orders subject to approval. Credit or debit balances in a customer's account(s) may be offset by any other outstanding balance owed by or to the customer. Please allow 4 to 6 weeks for delivery. Offer available while quantities last.

Your Privacy—Your information is being collected by Harlequin Enterprises ULC, operating as Reader Service. For a complete summary of the information we collect, how we use this information and to whom it is disclosed, please visit our privacy notice located at corporate.harlequin.com/privacy-notice. From time to time we may also exchange your personal information with reputable third parties. If you wish to opt out of this sharing of your personal information, please visit readerservice.com/consumerschoice or call 1-800-873-8635. **Notice to California Residents**—Under California law, you have specific rights to control and access your data. For more information on these rights and how to exercise them, visit corporate.harlequin.com/california-privacy.

HD20R2

IF YOU ENJOYED THIS BOOK
WE THINK YOU WILL ALSO LOVE

Escape to exotic locations where passion knows no bounds.

Welcome to the glamorous lives of royals and billionaires, where passion knows no bounds. Be swept into a world of luxury, wealth and exotic locations.

8 NEW BOOKS AVAILABLE EVERY MONTH!

Love Harlequin romance?

DISCOVER.

Be the first to find out about promotions, news and exclusive content!

f Facebook.com/HarlequinBooks

Twitter Twitter.com/HarlequinBooks

Instagram Instagram.com/HarlequinBooks

Pinterest Pinterest.com/HarlequinBooks

ReaderService.com

EXPLORE.

Sign up for the Harlequin e-newsletter and download a free book from any series at **TryHarlequin.com**

CONNECT.

Join our Harlequin community to share your thoughts and connect with other romance readers!
Facebook.com/groups/HarlequinConnection